Kitty Valentine
Dates Santa

Spin the wheel.
Date the guy.
Write the story.
Fall in love!

jillian dodd

Kitty Valentine dates Santa

JILLIAN DODD

Jillian Dodd, Inc.
Madeira Beach, FL
Jillian Dodd is a registered trademark of Jillian Dodd, Inc.

Editor: Jovana Shirley, Unforeseen Editing,
www.unforeseenediting.com

ISBN: 978-1-953071-99-6

Books by Jillian Dodd

London Prep
London Prep: Book One
London Prep: Book Two
London Prep: Book Three

The Keatyn Chronicles
Stalk Me
Kiss Me
Date Me
Love Me
Adore Me
Hate Me
Get Me
Fame
Power
Money
Sex
Love
Keatyn Unscripted
Aiden

Kitty Valentine Series
Kitty Valentine dates a Billionaire
Kitty Valentine dates a Doctor
Kitty Valentine dates a Rockstar
Kitty Valentine dates a Fireman
Kitty Valentine dates an Actor
Kitty Valentine dates a Best Man
Kitty Valentine dates a Cowboy
Kitty Valentine dates a Hockey Player
Kitty Valentine dates Santa

Chapter One

CHAMPAGNE IS ALWAYS a good idea. Especially when you're the perfect combination of incredibly happy and just tipsy enough not to be drunk. Matt and I are in the limo Grandmother insisted take us home tonight.

Tonight. I don't think the smile ever left my face. Grandmother is married, and I'm … well, I'm with Matt. We danced. And kissed.

He squeezes my hand. "What are you thinking about?"

"How we first met."

He chuckles. "You had all that alcohol, and I asked you if you wanted me to remember you in your bed. Dead. But when you asked if you would be naked, I will admit that my mind went places."

"What kind of places?" I flirt.

"Obviously of you in *my* bed. All sprawled out. I might have even wished for it." He laughs out loud. "Of course, then my wish came true. I learned very quickly that I needed to be more specific in my wishes."

"Oh, are you referring to the night you opened

the door, wearing nothing but workout pants? You were slightly out of breath. A little sweaty. I forgot why I was there."

"I noticed. You were totally checking out my body. Of course, you were shit-faced. I just didn't know it yet."

"I asked you what your favorite position was. You said you'd have to show me."

"And you told me it was for research. Speaking of that …" He pulls me closer and puts his lips on mine.

Which is a wondrous feeling, but I can't help but be surprised by it. This is Matt. My neighbor, who I lived next door to for a year and only admired from afar. At least he has no idea about that.

"Speaking of what?" I ask coyly in between kisses, wondering if he's going to bring up his favorite position.

"I read *Candy-Coated Love*."

Oh. Shit.

"And I was thinking that the golden retriever in the book sounded a lot like Phoebe."

"Probably," I try to say nonchalantly. "I am inspired by everyday events. I've always thought that she's a pretty dog."

"And what about the guy?" He leans back, gives me a smirk, and speaks in a girlie voice, "*A six-foot-plus mountain of lean muscle with a perfect smile, who looks like a fairy-tale prince and has an adorable, playful dog.*"

"You memorized the book?"

"Not the book, just that part. And the fact that they live across the hall from each other. Admit it—you've been crushing on me this whole time."

I should deny it. But I'm done fighting with him. "It's all true."

"Excellent," he says. "Because I was thinking about candy-coating myself later."

"Excuse me?"

"You like chocolate, right? And I was hoping that, tonight, I could talk you into coming to my place." And just when I think, Oh, that's so sweet, literally, he cracks a grin. "Maybe we could do it in the missionary position?"

"Ah! That was a low blow! You can't use my stories against me."

"Oh, really?" He laughs. "It's because of the book that I have chocolate. And champagne chilling. Rose petals on the bed. I'll bring you coffee and breakfast in the morning—just like your hero did in the book."

I falter for a moment as the story comes back to me.

"I want that again," I blurt out.

"Wait?! The book wasn't about me? Shit."

"Oh no. It *totally* was about you, but that's not what I meant. I know the sexy stuff is selling, and I know it was good for me to get out there, but it's not what I want to write. I like crafting sweet stories where I focus on a couple's relationship, not their

3

sex life. The kind of book where you can feel their love through the pages."

"Then, that's what you should do. Which works out for me because I'd like to date you, Kitty. *Just you*. And I feel like that would be hard to do if you were dating guys for research."

"But back to the candy-coated part," I say, quickly changing the subject.

He looks down the front of my dress and grins. "Does that mean you'll come over tonight, Valentine?"

"I will. And who knows? With enough champagne, maybe I'll reenact the *first* night I slept in your bed."

"Minus the puking," he says.

"Deal."

SOMETIME VERY EARLY in the morning, before the sun is up, I do wake up in a similar fashion to that first time—my eyes coming to rest on a naked shoulder next to me.

To a dog who barks the second I move.

"How are you feeling?" Matt asks with a knowing look.

Only this time, he's not referring to the fact that I was drunk. He's referring to the fact that last night was hands down the best night of my life. The best sex of my life.

"Perfect," I say dreamily. "The chocolate was amazing."

"Oh, break my heart. Surely, that wasn't the *only* thing that was amazing."

"Hmm," I tease. "Let me think about it. I did enjoy doing a little striptease for you."

He pulls me closer to him, allowing me to feel his naked body against mine—and one part in particular seems to be standing at attention.

"I enjoyed that as well."

I expect him to tease me a little, but instead, he bends down and kisses my forehead. A total boyfriend move.

"I loved everything about last night." He takes a deep breath and then says, "And I'm pretty sure that I love you, Kitty Valentine."

If I were writing this scene in a book, my heroine's breath would catch, and she would shed a tear, saying something perfectly romantic back. But this isn't a book. It's my life.

I mean, I do breathe in. I do find tears pooling in my eyes. And I say the only thing I can think of, "On the rooftop."

"Um, what?"

And I know what he's thinking. *What the hell is she even talking about?* And I know what I should say, but it's just jumbled up because I'm feeling slightly woozy and warm inside. *Is this what real love or true love feels like?*

"On the rooftop. My rooftop party. I, um … you asked me if I knew what I was going to wish for. I wished for this. *For you.*"

"Really?"

"Yep."

"Does that mean I don't have to make break-fast?"

"Oh no. That's so I'll keep you."

"And what do you have to do to *keep* me?"

I roll my eyes and don't reply. I don't need to. I just reach down under the covers and let my hand answer his question.

I FEEL SOMETHING wet and cold against my hand, which is hanging off the edge of the mattress. It takes me a moment to realize it's Phoebe. I reach down, smile at her, and give her head a pat.

I roll over, wondering why she's out of her kennel, and realize that Matt isn't in bed with me. For a second, I almost wonder if everything that happened last night was just some amazing dream.

But then he walks in the room. Shirtless, carrying a tray of food.

God, does it get any better than this?

But it does—when he smiles at me.

"I thought the smell of coffee might wake you," he says.

"Phoebe thought it was time I got up."

"She's raring to go. I took her outside real quick when I got up, but I wasn't going to leave you long enough to take her for our usual walk."

"I wouldn't have minded."

"I know you, Kitty," he says. "You would have

freaked out when I was gone and thought I was trying to get away from you."

"Well, you *have* hidden in my apartment before to get away from a few girls."

"True, but this is now." He sets the tray on my lap and then gets back into bed with me. "I told her we'd go for a long walk later. Don't forget, you're supposed to meet Hayley for brunch this morning."

"Oh shit. What time is it?"

"Nine. You aren't meeting until eleven, right?"

I let out a sigh of relief. "Yes, that's right."

"And we worked up an appetite last night. So, eat."

I can't help but smile. "Yes, we did."

We relax in bed, lazily eating. Drinking our coffees, chatting about nothing but the weather. I'm acting all calm and cool, but I am internally trying to decide how to get out of brunch.

I can't go to brunch.

Not now. Not when I finally got to sleep with Matt.

Not after he told me he's pretty sure that he loves me.

Because I don't ever want to spin that stupid wheel again.

"I'M NOT FEELING great," I lie. "I think it was the champagne. I'm going to call Hayley and cancel."

Matt suggestively slides his hand up my inner thigh. "Are you sure it's not just because you want to stay here in bed with me all day?"

Oh. That's an even better idea than pretending to be sick.

I grin at him. "That's *exactly* what I want. I just need an excuse."

"Tell her where you are. Right now. That you're naked. She'll understand," he says with a smirk.

I sigh. "I know she would, but I'm not sure I want to tell her just yet."

"She's your best friend. You tell her everything."

"It's new, Matt. This. Us. I'm just not ready to tell her." Or admit that it's really real. I'm afraid if I say it out loud, I might break the spell.

"Do you think she'll be surprised?"

"Probably not. It's just that … I'm supposed to spin the wheel."

"Oh, that," he says, nodding his head.

"Yes, that," I reply, waiting on bated breath to hear his reaction. To have him tell me he doesn't ever want me to spin that thing again.

"Then, you definitely have to go."

"Wait. What? You're okay with me dating someone else?"

"Let's cross that bridge when we get there," he says, patting my butt and shooing me out of his bed. "I'm sure we can work something out."

Work something out?

"Since it's for your job and all."

And I'm a little troubled by this. Because if I can date, so can he.

Chapter Two

THERE'S GOT TO be some sort of award coming my way. Like a Nobel Prize or something. Whatever they give to people who somehow manage to drag themselves out of bed, away from an incredibly sexy man—the man they have been drooling over forever—to have brunch with a friend.

I go over to my apartment and tousle my hair, and I'm totally surprised by how good I look. How happy. I get dressed and am ready in no time because I know that the sooner I get this over with, the sooner I can get home and back *into* bed with Matt.

Like, if he wants to hang out with me some more.

Now that I think about it, he didn't say anything about later.

Oh well. Don't care. I'm going over there and offering myself up for another night of sexual fun.

AS I ENTER the restaurant, Hayley waves at me from a booth against the wall.

I get a quick look-over and a low whistle.

"Wow. You look great."

She knows. Does she know?

I slide into the booth, settle in, and wonder why she chose this diner instead of her preferred fancy brunch place. Although, based on the aroma, I can probably guess why. It smells amazing.

"This is why we are friends," I tell her. "You always make me feel good."

"Or was it Matt?" she asks, cutting straight to the point.

"Um, uh," I stutter. *Come on, Kitty. Tell her. You're dying to.* "What makes you say that?"

"You were dancing pretty close at the wedding," she says, studying me. "You looked like a couple in love. I hoped that might transition into the bedroom."

I'm trying to decide what to say when our waiter asks if we are ready to order.

"Coffee?" I ask Hayley.

"Hair of the dog is what the doctor ordered. Turns out, I overindulged a little last night. Thus, our brunch spot for this morning." She turns to the waiter and holds up two fingers. "Bloody Marys, please."

"You don't look hungover," I say, noting her sparkling eyes. "You just look in love."

"I'm not actually hungover. Just hungry. Starving actually." She gives the waiter a toss of her hair and says, "We'll figure out our order while you grab our drinks."

He leaves, and we peruse the menu in silence for a moment.

When she sets her menu down, she says to me, "I am in love. Very in love. Isn't it so fun that we're in love at the same time?"

"Have I actually admitted to being in love with Matt?"

"You don't have to. I already know."

Our drinks are set in front of us, and let me tell you, they are huge.

"This is like brunch in a drink. Do we even need to order?" I say with a laugh as I take in all the things skewered on a stick.

"It's supposed to be the biggest Bloody Mary in town. I suppose I could let you read about it, but it's more fun to tell you. This delightful drink in front of you," she says, mimicking a salesperson, "has organic vodka, Bloody Mary mix, a jumbo shrimp, a slice of bacon, a beef stick, some peppers and olives, and two cream cheese–filled celery sticks."

"You want to order?" our waiter asks, causing us to realize he's still there.

As per usual, Hayley doesn't miss a beat. "I'll have the lobster grilled cheese and sweet potato fries."

"And I'll have the cheeseburger and rosemary truffle hash browns."

The second he's gone, Hayley holds her drink up in the air. "A toast," she says. "To friends, great loves, and of course, books."

"Books?"

She takes a sip of her drink and a bite of bacon before nodding her head and saying, "Yes, books. Don't forget, today's the day. We have to spin. You have a call with Maggie tomorrow still, right?"

"Right," I say, my stomach sinking. *Is Matt really going to be cool with me dating someone else, even in the name of research?* The thought distresses me. "You surprise me, Hayley."

"Why's that?"

"Because you usually get something healthy, like avocado toast or an egg-white-omelet type thing."

She waves her hand through the air and picks up her drink again, taking a big gulp. "I decided it was a cheat day. Make that, a whole cheat weekend. I think I ate my body weight in stuffed mushrooms and desserts at the wedding last night. I could barely button my jeans this morning." She arches an eyebrow. "So, I notice you didn't argue about my using the words *great loves* in our toast."

"Aren't we a little old for word games?"

"If it means that you're getting used to the idea of being head over heels in love. So, come on. Spill. Tell me what happened last night."

"We danced."

"I mean, *after* the reception. Want to know what Nicholas and I did?"

"You went home and had sex?"

"For a romance writer, that was a pretty boring

way to put it. For your information, we did go home and have sex. But sex with him is more than just a good time in bed. He's amazing. We're incredible together. Every. Single. Time."

"Fine. I'm in love with Matt. There. I said it."

"Sorry, sorry, but what? Did you just say that? You're admitting you have feelings for him?"

"Yes, okay? I'm in love with Matt. With my annoyingly hot neighbor who makes fun of me all the time."

She props up her chin on her palm, batting her eyelashes. "Also the Matt who takes care of you when you're sick."

"And who has an adorable dog. He's the full package. I just don't know," I admit.

And I know what's going on. Even though last night was amazing, I'm freaking out a bit. I love him. And now, I'm about to spin the wheel. And he's okay with it.

"Don't know what?"

"If I'm enough for him," I practically whisper. "You should have seen the girls he brought home. They were all beautiful. And a lot of them were really nice. I'm … just a mess. Always."

She sighs. "I knew we'd get to the heart of it eventually. It's scary. I know that. I mean, here I am, wondering if Nicholas and I have what it takes to justify a move across the country. I'd be leaving behind everything I've ever known."

Is it a coincidence that she drains what's left of

her drink moments after she finishes speaking? I'm guessing not. And I'm instantly worried about her. Now that I take a good look at her, I notice she doesn't look as pulled together as usual. And it's not her typical work stress. She's happy but stressed about her life.

"What are you going to do?" I ask her.

"I haven't made up my mind yet," she says. "And it's so stressful. But I think I need to move with him regardless of if they give me my transfer. Because it's what my heart wants. Even if my head has a million reasons why it's a stupid idea. And my parents will freak, knowing that I'm giving up my job at a highly regarded firm for the unknown. They will say I'm ruining my life for a man. They will ask me, *What happens if it doesn't work out?*"

"And what if it doesn't?" I ask and then realize that was the wrong thing to say. "I don't mean that I think it won't. I think you and Nicholas are meant to be together. I just meant, like, what's the worse-case scenario? It doesn't work, and you come back home. You could live with me or your sister if you needed to. I'll always help you. You know that, right? And even though the thought of not having the option of brunch with you every weekend makes me really sad, I understand."

"Oh, don't say that. You're going to make me cry," she says, sounding choked up. But then she shakes her head at me and says, "Before I go though, we have to figure out your life."

"One interesting thing did happen last night. Matt told me that he read *Candy-Coated Love*."

"Ohhh, that's the one that's basically about him and Phoebe, right?" she says as our food arrives and we start eating.

"Yeah, but it got me thinking."

"Uh-oh," she says with a laugh.

"I miss it. I miss writing those kinds of stories. The meet-cutes. The first time they hold hands. Kiss. All those sweet little moments that show their love outside of the bedroom. Or wherever."

"Then, do it. Maggie has to know that you can't keep dating guys for research for the rest of your life. Especially if you and Matt are together."

"Whatever happened to letting nothing stand in the way of my career?"

"I don't know. I guess my opinion has changed."

"Because you have Nicholas now."

She arches an eyebrow. "That could be. You're probably right about that. Oh my God. I'm doing that, aren't I? All the things I said you should never do. I'm giving up my career for a man. What is wrong with me?"

"You're maybe, possibly giving up your job, not your career," I say, but I can tell she's freaking out. "You'll still be an attorney either way."

"I need to be bold. And so do you. Talk to Maggie about what you want to write. Because why can't you just write from your imagination?"

"I don't know. But I get the idea she's stressed about her job, and she's afraid to change things up. Maybe she's superstitious." I pick at the rest of my hash browns, which are delicious.

"Well … you still need to spin to decide the next book, but you need to be a big girl and tell her that this is the last one. That you will either continue to do tropes but not spin or date or you will go back to writing what you want."

"That's easier said than done, you realize," I counter. "I've saved some money from my advances, and I'll have royalties coming in for most of my life, but without new releases, those will wither down to nothing."

Out comes the spinner regardless.

"We both need to figure out how to balance our careers with what we want out of life."

"Do you have any answers?" I say, taking a big gulp of my drink.

"I wish I did. But I'm leaning toward love."

"OKAY, LET'S GET it over with. Do you think we can manage one more?" Hayley asks.

"We?" I wonder.

"Okay, me. But I need the moral support," I say.

"Kitty, you don't have to keep doing this if you don't want to. It's up to you."

"Just spin it. For me."

"I have a good feeling about this one." She taps her fingers on the table and hops up and down a little.

"What did you do to it this time?" And I can't help but wonder if she rigged it like she had for the best man.

"Nothing." She presses her lips together in a thin line and looks down at the table.

"Lies." *Is it my imagination, or is she softly humming "Jingle Bells"?* My eyes narrow. "Wait. You didn't."

She sets the spinner moving with an ear-to-ear smile. I can only close my eyes and pray for strength at this point.

"Oh my goodness, Kitty! You got Hot Santa!"

"No."

"Yes!"

"Hayley, I can't date Santa."

"And why not?" she asks.

"Because he was an addition—by you! And the real Santa isn't even located in New York. He's at the North Pole. Everyone knows that."

"It will be fun," Hayley pleads.

"I hate you so much," I say with a grin.

"You have to date Santa. You have to date Santa," she says in a singsong voice. "Finally! I get my wish!"

"What does any of this have to do with you?"

"I just want to say my best friend dated Santa. What's wrong with that?"

"Uh, for starters, most men who play Santa aren't exactly young. Or attractive."

"How would you know? Do you troll Santa actor websites in your spare time?"

I roll my eyes. "Oh, yes. It's how I like to unwind."

"We'll figure something out. Leave it to me."

I love her. I trust her.

But I doubt even my amazing bestie can figure this one out.

Especially since I haven't told her about what really happened with Matt last night.

And again this morning.

Chapter Three

MONDAY MORNING CAME a lot faster than I'd expected.

Probably because that's basically all I did yesterday. *Get it? In bed. With Matt.*

Whatever.

Right now, I have some things I need to discuss with Maggie.

I wrote them down on paper and have them in front of me so that I don't get distracted.

TELL MAGGIE THIS. BE FIRM. BUT POLITE.

** I will not date for research anymore.

** I want to go back to writing the stories in my heart, whether they sell or not.

And I'm a little nervous because Maggie is so … Maggie.

"Maggie! How are you?" I ask when she answers, sounding more chipper than I feel.

"What do you want, Kitty?"

"Um, we had a call scheduled for today."

"Yes, I know that. But I can tell from the tone of your voice that you have something to discuss besides your next book."

"Well, now that you mention it—"

I can picture her in her office, leaning back in her chair with all of Manhattan spread out behind her. I always wonder why she doesn't turn her desk, so she can take in that view every day. Who knows? Maybe when she's on calls like this, she swivels around in her chair. She's definitely impeccably clothed and groomed. She's sort of like my grandmother in a way. Polished and elegant.

I clear my throat and get started. "So, there's a problem with this whole trope thing."

"The last time I checked, that *trope thing* is the reason your books are selling."

Nothing like a thinly veiled threat to start a conversation.

"You're right, and it was a genius idea. Like I said, I know how much I owe you. But …"

"I knew this was coming," she says, but I keep going.

"It might be nice if I didn't have to keep dating around." I look down at my list, knowing I'm already failing to make my first point clear. But I'm trying to ease her into this. *That's right. Take it slow. Make her think it's her idea.*

She lets out a frustrated sigh. "We've been over this before, Kitty."

"I know we have, Maggie. I was there."

If she thought my response was a little snarky, she chooses to ignore it, saying simply, "Then, you know how I feel. This has been a good thing for your career, in case you've already forgotten. And maybe you did forget. All you have to do is sit in your apartment in your pajamas and make up stories all day while *I* have to do everything else."

Wow. I never expected her to say something like that. Especially in that tone. I get it from others. People who don't understand how hard it is to write a book. The commitment it takes. The tenacity. But to hear it from her, someone in the industry who knows the work involved, really upsets me. I don't even know how to reply.

But I don't have to because she's apparently not done yet. "*Some of us* have to get up and go into the office every day and deal with the business side of things. The editing, the covers, the marketing, the printing, the distribution. We do *all* the things that get your books in the hands of readers. And all you have to do is go on a few dates and write about them. What a nightmare that must be."

"Okay, I get it." I take a deep breath.

Maggie has never treated me like this. I don't understand. *Where's Lois when I need her? Or do I need her? This is bullshit. I should stand up for myself.*

"No, actually, Kitty, I don't think you do. Do you know *anything* about the current state of publishing? How tough times are? Do I have to remind you, yet again, just how lucky you are to have a contract with a publisher who keeps throwing money at you?"

"I'm assuming the only reason you are throwing money at me is because my books are selling. And *you* are making money off me, the person sitting in her apartment, making up stories all day. You might own the rights to sell my books, but you don't own me." *There. Take that.*

Maggie sighs heavily again. "Book sales are down across the board. You're lucky that you are doing well. Do you understand what I'm saying? Stick to what works."

"I can make up what works! That's what I'm trying to say. I know the formula now. Dating around for inspiration was necessary at first—I'll give you that. But things have changed. I've written eight books based on my dating life, but a lot of it was flat-out made up. I never actually did it in an elevator *or* in an alley, but I wrote about it like I had. Do you not have faith in me as a writer anymore?"

"I have nothing but faith in you. It's everyone else I have a problem with," she says with a snarl.

Gee. Someone is having a bad day. Is that all this is? Is she just taking it out on me?

"I'm sorry that things aren't going well for you, Maggie," I say, softening a little. "I really am. But I'm going to be clear about one thing: I am not going to date for the sake of my next book."

"Who is it?" she says in an accusatory tone, sounding more like the Maggie I know so well.

"What do you mean?"

"Is it that neighbor of yours? I knew it was only a matter of time."

"You did?"

"So, it *is* him?"

"It doesn't matter *who* it is, Maggie. That's the point. It's personal. I'll write about anything you want, but this is nonnegotiable," I say firmly. *Oh, I almost sounded like Hayley there. Go me.*

Maggie is quiet for a long time.

Too long.

"Anything else you want to discuss?" I ask.

"Actually, there is. I was hoping to discuss this in a face-to-face meeting in my office."

Shit. This doesn't sound good.

"You know your books have a healthy marketing budget."

"Yes," I say tentatively.

"The traditional way of marketing a book has shifted. We used to do press releases and things like that. Now, it's all about influencers. A few days ago, I suggested that we play up the real-life angle regarding you. That we allow your readers—and more importantly, those who haven't yet read you—to hear how you have used writing these tropes as somewhat of a social experiment. The team loves the idea, and we feel it will boost your sales to new heights."

"You know I'm not a fan of interviews, Maggie."

"I know you want to keep your personal life private. I get that. But the thing is, if this plays out the way we think it will, you could *literally* become a real-life Carrie Bradshaw. *A successful young woman in New York City navigates the dating scene* kind of thing. I've never seen the marketing department so excited."

My heart practically stops. *I could be a real-life Carrie Bradshaw?*

"Of course, confidentiality as to who you've dated would be a priority," she adds. "And because I know you don't like the idea of going on television, we thought we'd start with influencer interviews, phone calls with journalists, that sort of thing, who will write articles about you. What we should have done was have you blog about this from the beginning, but whatever. What you should care about is the publicity you will get. Your books will sell like hotcakes. You'll reach a whole new market."

And I realize this is my chance to get what I want. I look down at number two on my list. "Fine. I'll do it."

"Oh, Kitty. Thank you. I know you will not re-gret—"

"On one condition," I add.

"What's that?"

"I write one more trope book. I do the publicity tour. And then I go back to writing whatever my heart desires."

"I'm not sure I can agree to that. It just wouldn't make sense. To build you up and then have you stop writing the tropes."

"Sorry. But that's my offer. Take it or leave it.

And I want it in writing."

"Kitty, I'm afraid I can't do that. But you have my word. Now, onto the fun stuff. Who will you be dating this time?"

"I spun the wheel at brunch yesterday and got Santa. Hayley's been wanting me to date Santa ever since we started doing this. And it's the right time of year to write about something like that."

"Oh, a holiday novel. Hmm. I'm not sure that will work though. We usually release holiday novels in the early fall."

"Save it for next year then," I say, really not caring anymore.

She agreed. I actually got her to agree.

"I'll tell you what. If you write fast and send me a few chapters at a time, maybe we could do a surprise digital release. That might be fun. We've never done that before."

"Sure. No problem," I say, knowing I'm going to need to start binge-watching Santa movies.

"Well then," Maggie says, "it was lovely speaking with you today, Kitty. This is going to be bigger and better than anything you've ever imagined. I can just see the ads now. A very Kitty Christmas. All right, I'm off. Got to get marketing going on this, stat."

And then she hangs up.

It sounds silly, but because I was so nervous about my call with Maggie, I did my makeup, fixed my hair, and put on a cute sweater dress. I consider going across the hall to see what Matt's up to and to tell him the good news—and possibly attack that fine body of his—but I know he's busy working, and I need to respect that.

So, holiday movies, here I come.

SIX HOURS AND a bowl full of popcorn and a bag of licorice later, I've got a notepad filled with plot ideas, and I'm feeling pretty pleased with myself. I'll never forget when this all started and Hayley first showed me the spinning wheel.

Another option caught my eye. "Hot Santa?"

She waved a hand at me. "I added that. I thought it would make a fun holiday edition. Plus, you'll get to sit on Santa's lap and tell him what a naughty girl you've been."

"Do you have any idea what the chances are of actually finding a hot Santa?" I asked with a giggle. "Maybe a dancer in a Santa costume but the type you see at the mall? Normally not that hot."

"You're the writer." She shrugged as our burgers arrived. "You'll figure it out."

And I think I actually have.

I was sort of stuck on the idea of dating, like, the real Santa Claus. Going to the North Pole with the elves and the reindeer, but making that sexy just didn't really fit. I'm pretty sure Mr. and Mrs. Claus don't have sex because, otherwise, they would have children, and he wouldn't have to live forever.

And then I remember when Bryce dressed up as

Santa at the firehouse last year to hand out presents. And I think that will be my angle. Hero of the book is dressed as Santa for a charity event. He meets the heroine in a cute way—maybe she spills a drink on him like that girl did to Paxton. She later ends up sitting on his lap and telling him a secret wish. Something she needs for her sick mother perhaps. Whatever—something heartwarming. And on Christmas Eve, he will fulfill her wish, dressed as Santa. And they will kiss. And now, you know they will be together forever. Which is really a good jumping-off point. Because it will take my readers back to the sweeter version of me before I actually go back to writing it. This book will definitely be the sweetest of all the trope books. I think it has to be. Because even though Bryce was sexy under the suit, I just—

Cannot.

Picture.

Doing *it* with Santa.

And I hope Maggie can understand that.

I'm getting up to grab my laptop when there's a knock at the door.

"Ho, ho, ho," I hear along with the sound of jingling bells.

I swivel my head from the door toward the television, wondering if I hit the wrong button and didn't shut it off. But the screen is blank.

"Weird," I say to myself. But then I hear it again. A knock.

And more *ho, hos.*

I fling open the door to find Matt and Phoebe. Phoebe looks adorable in a red Santa hat with white fur trim and a jingle-bell collar around her neck. She's wagging her tail, and she wants me to pet her, but I can scarcely move.

Because Matt is dressed up too. His hat matches Phoebe's. There's a fake mustache and beard combination carelessly hanging around his neck. My eyes trail down to his naked chest, washboard stomach, and deep V line. The only thing covering his upper half is a pair of red suspenders decorated with little red-and-white Christmas trees. Further down are red velvet pants with white fur cuffs and shiny black shoes.

I'm pretty sure drool is coming out of my mouth. It's definitely hanging wide open at the sight of him.

"What are you doing?" is all I can think to say because scratch my earlier plot.

I want to do sexy things to this Santa. I want to jingle his bells, sit on his lap, and tell him just how naughty I want to be. I want to talk about big packages, unwrapping his gifts, and going down the chimney. I want to lick his candy cane, make him come to town, and be his Vixen.

Matt gives me a wide grin and then says, "A little birdie told me you needed some inspiration. Figured this might be better than you trolling the malls."

"Oh, Santa baby," I say, pulling him inside before pushing him onto the couch and taking a seat on his lap.

Kris showed up at her door, wearing only part of a Santa suit. His naked chest glistened with new-fallen snow, indicating that he had driven all the way over there in his red Ford sleigh like this to see her. When they had talked about having a cozy night of drinking hot chocolate by the fire, this was not what she'd had in mind.

But she'd take it.

"Have you been a good little girl this year?" he said to her, a grin playing across his face.

I've been really good this year, *she thought.*

At least, she had been until Kristopher—Kris for short—rode up on his motorcycle a week ago, stopped in front of her gift shop, shook his long hair out of his helmet, and strode inside. He was a man who had moved with purpose that day, looking for Christmas cookie exchange invitations for his mother.

"I had been until you showed up, Santa," she cooed. "Now, I plan on being very, very naughty."

Kris swept her off her feet and carried her over to the fire. She'd spent hours setting the perfect scene—a roaring fire, plaid blankets and holiday pillows spread across the floor, a tray of fresh gingerbread cookies she'd spent the morning baking and decorating, peppermint schnapps–spiked hot chocolate in a thermos, and Santa mugs with marshmallows already in them—imagining a sweet, romantic night of cuddling and getting to know each other.

When he set her on the floor, she reached up and grabbed his neck, pulling him to her lips. He kissed her in a way that was almost violent, his desire apparent. She was pushing the suspenders holding up the Santa pants off his shoulders while he unbuttoned the ugly green garland cardigan sweater that she was wearing before tossing it somewhere.

"Santa approves of this," he said, running his hand across the red silk camisole she'd also carefully picked out. You know, just in case. "Very festive. Want to jingle my bells?"

She didn't bother to answer, just slipped her hand inside his Christmas tree-covered boxers. He really had gone all out on this. For her.

And it made her love him even more.

Which was crazy. She'd only known him for a week. She'd never fallen in love in a week. Never even considered sleeping with someone she'd known for such a short time. Maybe it was just the holiday spirit or the fact that he was the sexiest man—and Santa—ever, but she did.

She'd had lovers before, but they were nothing like this. Everything was surprising, like how effortlessly he pulled her onto his lap. The funny little sexual jokes he made about his big package and giving her a gift. And the pleasure she felt.

They had sex. Naughty Santa sex for a long while, never able to get enough of each other. But later, after they finally remembered the cookies and hot chocolate and ate a few, they made love. Slow, sweet, tender, and utterly incredible love.

He was still inside her when he ran his fingers through her hair and whispered, "I love you, Kitty. I want you to meet my family."

Oh crap.
Backspace. Backspace. Delete.

He was still inside her when he ran his fingers through her hair and whispered, "I love you, Mary. And I want you to meet my mother."
He reached for the Santa pants that were flung over a nearby chair and pulled out an invitation. The one he'd bought at her store. Inviting her to his mother's cookie exchange.

"How's it going?" Matt asks. It's nearly four in the morning, and he is lying across my bed, the sheet not covering much and seriously distracting me even though he's been asleep for a few hours.

"I wrote, like, a gazillion words," I tell him. "Thank you for letting me get it all down. I had so much in my head, just screaming to come out."

He raises his eyebrows and chuckles at me.

"You, Santa," I say, quickly hitting Save on my manuscript before sauntering over to him, "have a dirty mind."

"And if you want Santa to bring you any presents this year, you're going to have to be very nice to him."

I jump on the bed, give him a passionate kiss, and notice his *North Pole* springing to attention.

Chapter Four

I WAKE UP but don't bother opening my eyes. I'm not ready to yet, and there's soft snoring coming from behind me. I can tell there is sunlight streaming in through the windows and am surprised that Matt would still be in bed at this hour.

I squint open one eye, glancing at the clock and seeing that it's nearly noon.

Which causes me to freak out, wondering if he's okay. Like, surely, I didn't kill my sexy Santa. Or he didn't die in his sleep.

Oh wait. I hear snoring. He's not dead.

Wake up, Kitty.

I roll over, putting my arm around him, planning to snuggle up with him. Only I connect with fur.

"Phoebe! What are you doing on the bed?" I say.

Matt is pretty strict about that with her.

She replies by rolling over, licking my face, and letting me scratch her belly.

"You were a cute elf yesterday," I say in the high-pitched voice I seem to only use when I'm talking to her. "Sorry I didn't tell you. Your dad distracted me."

I expect her to give me another kiss, but instead, her body jerks still, her nose goes up into the air, and she sniffs. She jumps off the bed, flies out of the bedroom, and starts scratching at my door.

But then I hear my apartment door open and Matt's voice talking softly to her, quickly followed by the smell of my favorite food.

"You got Chinese?!" I yell out.

"Don't move," he says. "I'm bringing it to you."

A few moments later, he comes into my room with a heap of food spread out on a tray.

"You're my hero," I tell him.

He sets the tray down just as Phoebe jumps onto my bed.

"Phoebe!" he says sternly. "Get down. You know you're not supposed to get on Kitty's bed."

Phoebe does as she was told, but she doesn't look happy about it.

"I woke up next to her instead of you. She was sleeping in your spot. Snoring."

"You need to be firm with her."

"Hard to be firm when I'm sleeping. And don't be to upset. If I couldn't wake up with you, it was nice to have the company. Whatcha got there?"

"Lunch."

"You really are a good neighbor," I tease, leaning in to give him a kiss as he sits on the bed with me.

"So, does that mean you enjoyed Santa's visit?"

"Oh, very much so."

"Me too," he says, feeding me my first bite and then handing me the container. "Sesame tofu for you."

I love that he knows what I like. In fact, he knows me better than just about anybody but Hayley. What I'd like to do is forget about the food and wrap my legs around him, but this is important.

"I wanted to tell you something yesterday, but then you were Santa. Anyway, I had a call with Maggie. I told her I don't want to do tropes anymore."

That gets his attention away from his food. He lifts his head and looks at me, his brows raised. "Really? What did she say?"

"Well, it's sort of complicated. I negotiated. One more book, Santa—which is practically writing itself, thanks to you—and then I can go back to writing what I want."

"Why's that complicated?" he asks, taking another bite of rice.

By the time I'm finished explaining how things went with Maggie, he's gritting his teeth, and the muscles in his cheeks are jumping. "Unbelievable. I can't believe she threw you under the bus like that!"

"Did she really throw me under the bus? Does this count as bus throwage?"

"Joke about semantics all you want, but in the end, she just made a huge decision without discussing it with you first. I can't believe she would do that."

"Trust me, I've known her a lot longer, and I can't believe it either. Though I guess it makes sense in a way. It's not like she keeps me in the dark about how difficult things are for the entire industry. If anything, she talks about it enough that it makes me wonder if I should find a new career."

"That's still not an excuse! You can't let her walk all over you like that."

"You're right, but I got her to agree with me in the end. I turn in the Santa book and do the publicity stuff for her, and then I can go on and do what I want."

"What she did is unethical."

"Is it though?" I wonder.

She is trying to help my career. Hers too, obviously, but still.

"I guess I don't understand. Are you happy about this?"

"Endgame? Yes. Doing the interview stuff? Not so happy. I mean, hello, this is me we're talking about. I have a hard enough time in one-on-one conversations with people I actually know. How the heck am I supposed to get through an interview? I'll end up making a huge fool of myself, and then nobody will want to buy my books. The entire thing is going to blow up in all of our faces."

"That's my point." He cocks his head to the side like he doesn't understand. "But it's more than that.

A lot more."

"What do you mean?"

"People are going to gravitate toward your story. I'm sure your publisher has tons of public relations people who will spin this in whatever way it takes to make you go viral."

Viral. The word rings out like a gong in my head.

And it's not a nice sensation.

"I didn't think about that," I admit.

"Your books will probably sell better than they ever have, but good luck ever getting a minute to yourself. You'll be lucky if you aren't mobbed on the street."

"Now, *that,* I have a hard time believing." I can't help but chuckle softly. "I thought I was the one who usually imagined the worst-case scenarios. Aren't you usually the one who stays calm?"

"I don't usually have to worry about someone I care about having her life shredded by a bunch of people who only want to make a quick buck. They're not the ones who'll have to deal with people asking rude, uncomfortable questions. And if you start doing actual interviews, like the kind where your face is visible, you're going to be recognized."

"We live in New York City. Do you have any idea how many people live here?"

"Millions."

"I seriously doubt I'm going to end up famous,

Matt. Not, like, to the point where people are going to recognize me on the street. I'm more nervous about having to do interviews."

"I'm sure if it's what you decide to do, Maggie or Lois could coach you through the things you should talk about."

"Lois?" I have to snort. "I'm sure she forgets she even has a client. But she doesn't have any trouble taking a percentage of my royalties—that's for sure."

"Either way, somebody will help you. There's too much on the line for them to let you go out there and say whatever comes into your head. The way you make it sound, they're putting a lot of eggs in this basket."

"Lucky me."

"You'll be fine. You always end up landing on your feet." He smirks. "I guess the name Kitty suits you, come to think of it," he teases.

"Oh, Chinese food and bad puns. I love it."

"I love that you stood up to her. Or at least tried to," he says, taking my hand in his.

"You sure you're not just excited because I don't have to date anyone else?"

"What I don't like is that Maggie acts like they own you. And you allow it. No matter what you signed with them, they do not own you." He strokes his chin with a thoughtful expression. "It's a shame you don't know a lawyer who could maybe help you look over your contract and figure out whether it's possible to get out of it. Like a lawyer who happens to be your best friend and who works with tons of other lawyers."

"And I'm thinking, my other best friend—"

"Are you referring to me?" he says, moving the tray of food over to my desk before diving back in bed with me. "Your boyfriend? Your lover? Your Santa Claus?"

"My boyfriend. That makes me feel like a teenager."

His hand slides up under my shirt. "Is that good or bad?"

"I think we're more than that, Matt. In fact, I'm pretty sure I'm in love with you. Have been for a long time."

He smiles at me and kisses me deeply. "Pretty sure? Or sure?"

"Um, well, the other night you told me you were *pretty* sure. I'm reciprocating. But if you'd like to answer the question first, I'd be happy to reciprocate again."

"That's how it works in your romance novels, doesn't it? The guy always tells the girl first."

"Mostly, yes. Actually, always. At least so far. But maybe you'll inspire me to change that."

"I hope I inspire you to change a lot of things about your life in the near future, Valentine," he says. "And to answer the question, I'm positive that I'm crazy in love with you."

Chapter Five

"I'M JUST SUPPOSED to fill out answers to the questions they sent over?" I scroll down, down, down the list.

"Piece of cake, right?" Lois sounds downright proud of herself. "See, this interview thing isn't going to be such a big deal after all."

She's not wrong. My relief is very real as I sit and scan over the email I received this morning. They're all pretty much softball questions—whose idea this was, how did I feel about it. Obviously, I can't tell the full truth. I don't think my publisher or my editor would like it very much if I shared exactly what happened the day Maggie informed me that I would need to change my entire approach.

Nobody wanted to hear about a girl getting drunk just so she could write a sex scene and then throwing up in her neighbor's living room, stripping off all her clothes, and passing out in his bed. Not my proudest moment, not something I want to share with the world.

"Okay, I can do this. Let's try to encourage written interviews."

"I don't know, doll. I talked to Maggie, and she made it sound like the higher-ups want you to show your face around. I'm already fielding phone calls from a bunch of different networks."

I almost pass out at the word. "Networks? Like, actual channels with actual news shows?"

"What did you think this would mean?"

"I don't know. Bloggers? Review sites? That's what Maggie alluded to."

"I'm sorry, sweetheart. This is much bigger than that."

Yeah, no kidding. People keep telling me that.

"And you'll make plenty of dough from these interviews too. Don't worry about that."

"I wasn't exactly worried about that part."

She snickers loudly. "Well, aren't you lucky then? Because for lots of people, that would be their first concern. Making a little extra money on the side just for the sake of getting their bills paid."

She has a way about her, Lois does. She's good at making me cringe.

"You're right, of course. I'm just really nervous about being on camera, and I would rather avoid it. I'm not trying to sound ungrateful, trust me."

"Everybody's nervous about being on camera the first time. I had a client back in the '90s who threw up in a bucket between his feet not ten seconds before the show went live, and he ended up knocking it out of the park."

"Ooh, who was it?"

"That's not important—though you'd know the name if you heard it. My point is, you'll do just fine. I'll make sure to have a list of questions in front of me before the interview, so you can be prepared."

I can breathe a little easier now. "Okay. That sounds pretty good actually."

"Does that mean you feel better about this?" There's a motherly tone in her voice that makes me smile even though I can't help feeling like she's patronizing me just a little.

"Yes, Lois."

"Very nice. Now, I have to make a few phone calls on your behalf. You've certainly been making me earn my money lately."

Rather than remind her of how easy I've made her job over the years and how she's finally earning her keep, I thank her for her help and end the call. She's great, and she got me my first deal with the publisher, so I can't undervalue her contributions, but still, there have been times over the past year when I've wondered why she's even around.

Whatever. I need to answer these questions and get back to my writing. I swear, with Matt as my muse, the writing is going very well.

THE FIRST FEW are beyond easy.

What made me want to become a writer?

I type out a response to that, explaining how I always loved to read and to write and how disappointment in my own love life led me to create my dream man in my first book.

Boy, I was young and naive then. Fresh-faced, hopeful, bright, and shiny.

How did I score a book deal so easily?

This one I'll leave entirely up to the skill of my agent. Sure, I had to reach out and query her in the first place, but she was the one who did the work to find Maggie. I can't take credit for that.

By early afternoon, I'm halfway through my immediate, off-the-cuff responses and wondering if I should go back now to edit, to smooth things out a little, when my phone rings.

Seeing Hayley's name makes my heart leap into my throat.

"What's wrong?" I blurt out the second the phone is against my ear.

She never calls me at this time of day.

The first thing I hear is sniffling, which ratchets my anxiety up another million degrees.

"They're sending him back sooner than planned."

I close my eyes. "Sweetie."

"He wasn't supposed to go back until after the holidays, but apparently, they need him for something out there. It's so stupid." Her voice has a strange, echoing quality, so I imagine she's calling from the ladies' room at work.

"That is so wrong! I mean, your relationship aside, how can they expect somebody to just go at a moment's notice?"

"I don't know, but he has to be back in the office on Monday morning."

"I know you have vacation time saved up. Other than the wedding, you haven't taken any. Maybe you can go out there with him."

"Yeah, but then there's family stuff. My brother, Brandon, is going to the trouble of coming back from his research trip, and I don't want to miss seeing him. Plus, I know that would just cause a huge blowup with the family. I don't feel like having to go through that."

I've seen her family in action. I can only imagine the way they'd react if they found out she was skipping out on family holiday time to be with her boyfriend. Not that they would begrudge her the time spent with him, but they would definitely lay a big guilt trip on her.

"Sometimes, we have to make these uncomfortable decisions. Somebody's bound to be disappointed, no matter what we decide."

"Why can't this just be easy? Why am I not allowed to be happy?"

I've never heard her talk this way before. "Nobody says you're not allowed to be happy. You deserve it more than just about anybody I know."

"Then, why is this happening? God, Kitty, I'm so tired." She sounds like it too. Like she's about a few moments away from giving up.

"Sweetie, what else is going on? Is there something you're not telling me?"

Another few sniffles. "I think I'm burned out. I think that's the problem. I've been working eighteen-hour days nearly seven days a week for how long now?"

"That's true."

"What for? I'm waiting for somebody to tell me whether I'm allowed to follow the man I really, really care about across the country. Like, he could be the one. I've never said that about anybody before."

"I know. That's pretty huge."

"But here I am, dancing on their string. It's like it doesn't matter how much work I put into my job or how good I am at it. All they want to do is wring every last bit of energy out of me. I look at you, and I see the freedom you have …"

I have to bite my tongue since I know she's not in any mood to be contradicted, but I don't exactly have a ton of freedom. If I did, I would tell Maggie and Lois and whoever else was involved that they could take this interview thing and shove it.

"I just don't know what to do." She sounds so forlorn, so heartbroken, that it brings tears to my eyes. "And if all that isn't bad enough, I just found out that I'm pregnant."

"What? Oh my God. That's amazing!"

"No, it's not. I'm not married."

"Who cares? It doesn't have to be that way anymore."

"My family is going to freak!" she counters.

"They might be surprised, but your mom is

going to be so incredibly happy! Plus, you love him. You're in love. It's a love child. So romantic."

"Until I'm stuck alone with the baby, jobless, because I followed him to California, only for him to break up with me."

"Are you excited about the baby?"

"Of course I am. I've always wanted children. And Nicholas wants them too. But I'm not thrilled about the timing, and I don't know how he's going to react. Really, how much more can our relationship take?"

"I wish I were there, so I could give you a hug."

"Just talking helps." She sniffles and then seems to pull herself back together. "I'll figure it out. I always do. Oh, and my sister, Kylie, wants to throw a good-bye party for Nicholas on Saturday night. She and Zack finally moved into their new place uptown. And since Nicholas probably won't be here for the holidays, it's holiday-themed. Will you come?"

"Of course. I'll be there."

"Thanks. And as soon as I come to terms with it myself, I'll take a dozen more tests to make sure it wasn't a false alarm, and then I'll tell him. But please, don't tell anyone. Promise me?"

"I promise. And you know, anything you need, I'm here."

"Thanks. I'll see you at the party."

"Nothing could keep me away." And I mean it.

Once we're off the phone, I place an order for cupcakes to be sent to her office. Something tells me she could use some right about now.

I'm so excited for her, but I understand why she's scared about all this. In my books, I've only had one unplanned pregnancy, and the hero in the story took the news well. He was thrilled. But seeing it play out in front of me with my best friend, I realize that life probably doesn't always go that way. Because she and Nicholas are stressed as it is. They are making big decisions about their future together. And she is worried about her career. Now, throw in the responsibility of providing for a baby on her own, and I can see why's she so worried.

The second I saw her name on the phone, I wanted to tell her about what had happened after the wedding, about my sexy Santa Matt, but I'm glad I didn't blurt it out. There's plenty of time to tell her all that.

And to ask her to look over my contract.

I think about Hayley's problem. She's brilliant and a hard worker. Dedicated and devoted. If her firm won't let her transfer for the sake of her personal life, she should find another firm with people who appreciate her talent.

I guess I could say the same for myself.

If I don't like the way they're treating me, maybe it's time for me to find another publisher.

I look down at the last question on the list.

How do you feel about opening up your creative process for the world to see?

I can't help but chuckle darkly and think, *Honey, you don't want the honest answer to that question.*

Chapter Six

"FRANKLY, YOU HAVE the leverage in this situation."

Because Hayley still hasn't told Nicholas, I decided talking to her about my contract might help distract her. And one of Hayley's work friends overheard us talking and has inserted himself into the conversation. Normally, I would feel intruded upon, but right now, I'm feeling desperate for legal advice.

"How so?" I ask him.

He doesn't look much older than either Hayley or me, and he's a good-looking guy, but he's wearing one of those old-fashioned sweaters with the leather patches on the elbows, like he sees himself as an academic. An academic, hipster lawyer. What a combination.

He shrugs and removes his horn-rimmed glasses. I swear, all he's missing is a pipe dangling from his lips. It's almost enough to make me giggle, and I want to write a character like him in one of my stories.

"You're the name. Pretty soon, you'll be the face. If they're so eager to get you out there in front of the rest of the world, it means they need you. The more popular you become as you give these interviews, the more power you'll have."

I'm starting to understand. "So, what you're saying is, if I want to get out of this arrangement, going along with the interviews and publicity is the smartest route to take."

He taps a finger against the tip of his nose and says, "Absolutely."

"It's good advice," Hayley agrees, nodding her head. "They need you more than you need them."

We excuse ourselves, and I follow her into Kylie's spacious, modern kitchen. Their apartment is gorgeous, and although I do tend to order takeout a lot, I'd love to learn to cook in a place like this.

"Can you help me with the appetizers?" Kylie hands me a pair of pot holders and jerks her chin toward one of the two ovens mounted against the wall as we walk into the kitchen.

"Double ovens," I sigh. "I swear, if I had the time to bake, I would use the hell out of these."

Kylie laughs while rummaging around in the cabinet over the sink. "Honestly, that was a huge selling point for me. That and the his-and-hers bathrooms. No offense to my husband, but if I had to work around his schedule, we'd have a big problem. I swear, he takes longer in there than I do."

Zack overhears this as he enters the kitchen and grabs her by the waist. "I just want to look pretty for you."

She rolls her eyes and slaps at his hands, but I can see the very obvious love between them.

So can Hayley, and I can tell it's killing her. She's smiling, but the lines etched across her forehead tell a different story.

"That and the three bedrooms," Zack says. "If our parents had their way, we'd start filling this place with kids right away."

My eyes get huge, and I glance at Hayley, trying not to be obvious.

"That's true," Kylie says, rolling her eyes. "Mom has been on us about that since our wedding day."

"And now, you have the house to do it," Hayley says flatly, looking around, and I know she's wondering where in the world she's going to live. She has a beautiful, well-appointed apartment, but it's not big. But I guess babies aren't big either.

"Babies do come with a lot of stuff. Cribs. Strollers. Toys. I read somewhere that to raise a child is something like over a million dollars," Zack says. "I'm just not ready to sign up for that yet."

Hayley starts to turn green, so I change the subject.

"My grandmother and Peter are still on their honeymoon," I blurt out. "Spain currently."

"I would love to move to Spain. The whole idea of taking a siesta every day because you're sort of expected to?" Kylie crosses her hands over her chest and flutters her eyelashes. "The dream."

Hayley barks out a disbelieving sort of laugh. "You? Little Miss Type A? Have you even taken a nap since kindergarten?"

"Excuse me, but I'll have you know that I've been working on my life balance ever since the wedding." Kylie gives me a meaningful look that brings to mind how she almost fell apart in the days leading up to the wedding, and it tells me she still values the advice I gave her then.

Honestly, I was only trying to help her enjoy her wedding and not be so stressed, but I guess if she's carried it into the rest of her life, that's really nice. And again, it reminds me that I should take my own advice more.

We all turn to the sound of someone letting out a loud laugh and see Nicholas by the Christmas tree.

"He has a great laugh, doesn't he?" Hayley lets out a soft sigh as we stand there, watching him laugh over the conversation he's having.

"He does and a good sense of humor to go along with it. That's really important," I say.

"There's only one other person in the world who makes me laugh as much as he does, and that's you." She looks me up and down, arching an eyebrow. "And while you look pretty cute to-night …"

"Don't worry. I won't take it personally if you don't hit on me tonight. Or ever for that matter."

"I KEEP HAVING to remind myself that he won't be here for Christmas. Not that he was ever supposed to be, but I was kind of hoping …"

I put an arm around her shoulders and squeeze tight. "I know. You wanted to be out there."

Kylie and Zack each grab food and take it out to the living room, leaving us a little privacy.

"I know it's stupid." Her voice is shaky, and I squeeze harder in response. "But I was hoping we could at least have the ball rolling with the transfer by then. That I could be looking for an apartment out there if we didn't decide to live together right away. But I still haven't heard anything. And I still haven't told him. Even though all ten tests were positive. I've decided, regardless of his reaction or what it means for us, I'm having the baby. I'm actually coming around to the idea. I did well in law school and expect to have good recommendations from my firm. I'll be fine." She looks down at her stomach. "We'll be fine."

"Of course you will be. Don't give up hope on the transfer just yet. I know it sucks when things don't follow some timeline in our head, but that doesn't mean it's not going to happen." I lean in and whisper in her ear, "And if you don't mind some advice, don't waste the time you have with him now, thinking about the way you want things to be. Go be with him. Make the most of the time you have. And you really need to tell him."

Her shoulders slide back. Her chin lifts. "You're

right." Then, she looks at me, and her smile slips. "What about you?"

"What about me? I think I can handle mingling alone."

"All right. Just no sneaking out on me. You wouldn't want to anyway; there's a surprise coming later on."

"Are you going to tell everyone now? Here?"

"Oh my God, no. Are you kidding me? It's party-related. You know Kylie and Zack. You were at their wedding. They do everything big."

She heads straight over to Nicholas and wraps her arms around his waist. He kisses her forehead— I swear, I am such a sucker for that—before looking down at her with an expression I can only describe as love.

Hayley deserves this. I don't think I've ever wanted anything for somebody else quite so much in my life. Sure, I wanted Grandmother and Peter to be happy and was thrilled half to death when they decided to get married, but somehow, I want this even more.

Here's the thing: I don't really feel like walking around and mingling at this party. Nothing against anybody here. Far from it. They all seem like nice people, and Kylie is a very sweet sister for throwing a holiday event, especially for her sister's boyfriend.

Still, I don't really know anybody, and Kylie is way too busy, overseeing things, to have time for chitchat.

Which is why I decide to jump in and help her. There's Christmas music playing, fresh cookies and other red and green goodies scattered around, and lots of spiked hot chocolate.

"You don't have to do that!" Kylie catches up to me in the kitchen as I'm refilling a platter of sugar cookies.

"Please, let me do something. I want to help out."

"If you insist." She pulls a bag of ice from the freezer and pours it into a bucket. "Hayley tells me you have to start giving interviews."

"Up until now, I've only had to do either the kind where they send in their questions and I email them back or phone interviews. But tomorrow, I'll be on an actual television show. And I'm really nervous about it. I don't want to make a fool of myself."

"You don't give yourself nearly enough credit. You'll do fine. You'll have to talk for, what, four or five minutes at the most?"

"Do you know how long four or five minutes can stretch out when you're a deer in headlights?"

She winces. "Yeah, I see your point. But I still say you'll do just great. You're quite charming."

I hand the platter of cookies off to somebody offering to take them out to the living room, laughing as I do. "Now, that is a word I don't think anybody has ever used to describe me."

"Then, nobody else knows you." She gives me a

playful nudge as she passes me. "I swear, you are so hard on yourself."

"That's something your sister accuses me of pretty much all the time."

"Then, she's even smarter than I thought, which is saying something."

We both turn toward the front hall when the doorbell rings.

To my surprise and complete confusion, Hayley just about flies over to the door. "It's time for the surprise!" She throws me a knowing grin before flinging open the door.

"Ho, ho, ho!"

Oh my gosh. She totally planned this. Because here comes Santa Claus, decked out from head to toe. Everybody bursts out into laughter and applause at the sight of him, and immediately, people start taking pictures.

"Did Hayley tell you about my Santa book?" I mutter to Kylie, watching as Santa works the room. He's even wearing the big, bushy beard and little wire-rimmed spectacles.

Which is going to be awkward, having a Santa here. Mostly because I haven't had the heart to tell Hayley about me and Matt yet. Or that I already found my sexy Santa. Or that the book is almost already written. I invited Matt to the party. I thought it would be a good way to ease into the conversation, but he had some work crisis.

And now is probably not the time to spring the

news either. Not when she and her sister went to the trouble of hiring someone.

Kylie only shrugs with a smile before heading over and directing Santa toward a chair near the Christmas tree. "Here you go! Now, everybody can take a turn telling Santa what they want this year!"

I don't want to upset anyone, so I figure I might as well have fun with it. Especially since everybody else is lining up to take pictures and sit on Santa's lap.

"Come on. You'd better get in line! Santa doesn't have all night." Kylie isn't exactly gentle when she pushes me toward the line.

Hayley joins us, handing me a cup of spiked hot chocolate and looking down the line to where Santa's posing for pictures. "I couldn't help myself. When Kylie decided to throw the party for Nicholas, it just fit."

I want to tell her. I know I should. Right now.

"So, you had nothing to do with this party? She just moved in!"

"Okay, okay." She blows out a huge sigh. "It was a collaborative effort, and maybe I spent last night and today putting up the tree and the decorations and everything. So what?"

"I love you. That's what. You are a good friend."

"I love you, too." She takes my cup and guides me forward. "It's your turn."

I step up to the plate, so to speak, and hold my arms out to the sides. "I guess I'm up."

"Come on." Santa's voice is deep and booming as he pats his lap. Not a bad sign, though I get the feeling he's putting the voice on for show.

I also realize this Santa looks like he's built pretty well under that red suit. Although I wouldn't expect anything else from Hayley.

I settle down on his thigh.

"Do you want to know whether I've been a good girl this year?" I ask.

Santa's eyes twinkle. "I think I *know* the kind of girl you've been this year, Kitty."

Oh my God. It's Matt.

"You lied to me about work," I mutter to him.

"And apparently, you still haven't told anyone about us," he counters.

Chapter Seven

"KITTY"—HAYLEY NUDGES ME—"SURPRISE! It's your Santa!"

I jump off Santa's lap, freaking out. I'm upset with myself for not telling Matt why I haven't told anyone yet. Now, I'm sure he has to wonder if I'm even serious about loving him.

But it's so incredibly sweet that he came anyway.

I would have loved to shock Hayley by giving Santa a great big kiss. But now is not the time. Honestly, I'm not sure how I let myself get into these awkward situations. Always.

"Kitty?" Matt looks concerned now. He pulls the fake beard down under his chin. "What's wrong? Are you okay?"

I have to get out of this apartment. The balcony will have to do for now even though it's freezing outside. Fresh air might be just what I need anyway. Because Hayley is going to be mad at me. And I can't handle that.

There are murmurs all around me as I elbow my way through the crowd, but that doesn't matter. I don't even know most of these people.

"Kitty!" Matt's voice rings out behind me once I reach the balcony.

My arms immediately break out in goose bumps, and my teeth chatter, but the cold air brings a little clarity to my fuzzy brain.

"Hey." Before I know it, there's the top half of a red Santa suit being draped over my shoulders. "Why did you run off?"

"Because you did this."

"And why wouldn't I?"

I suddenly realize something. "Wait. Who was the little birdie who told you about me spinning Santa the other day?"

He grins. "It was Hayley—when she asked if I would come to this party, dressed as Santa. For you. But I figured, how much fun would that be? I mean, here, I wouldn't be able to do what I did to you then. At least, not right away."

"So, you already knew I hadn't told her about us. Why didn't you say something?"

"Kitty, in case you haven't figured it out, I've been in love with you since the night you stumbled across the hall with your laptop and made me read what you had written."

"I didn't make you. You read that on your own." *Crap. That's the wrong thing to say. For heaven's sake, how many scenes like this have I written?*

"What difference does it make? I fell for you, and I've been in love with you ever since then. Even when you drive me out of my mind. Even when you're stubborn. When you pick fights for no good reason. When you have to have the last word. My real dilemma though is that I'm in love with a girl who has to date random guys or else, I don't know, risk giving up her career. And I would never, ever ask you to do that. I want what you want. And I'm proud of you."

"You are?"

"Yes, I am." He reaches out to run a hand over my hair. And it feels good. "You're a hard worker. You're a talented writer. And you're a good friend. You have a huge heart, you're generous and thoughtful, and you support the people who matter to you."

I can't think of anything to say, so I shrug. Because even though we've slept together and we've said we love each other, we haven't talked about this. He hasn't told me all this. And I'm really touched.

My mouth opens. Then, it closes. "You'd think a writer would be able to come up with something to say in a situation like this."

He grins. "This isn't our happily ever after yet, so I'd go with something simple." His hands find my arms. "Why don't I give it a shot?"

"I'd like that." I take a step closer to him, the whole world fading away.

He purses his lips. "Hmm. I think the girl in the story would accept the fact that her totally awesome, freakishly handsome, wildly successful, wickedly funny, stallion-in-the-sheets neighbor is the *perfect* man for her."

"He does sound like the total package."

"He definitely is."

"He sounds pretty humble too," I tease.

"I'm only being honest," he banters back. "What's the saying about life imitating art?" He pulls me closer still, until I'm up against his chest. "The fact is, I'm completely crazy about you, and I have been for a long time. And if the only thing keeping us from being in a committed relationship is your work, I'm willing to wear a Santa suit in front of a bunch of strangers for the sake of being with you."

"You forgot to add that he is really sweet," I say.

"Gosh, how did I forget sweet? That's why you started writing romance in the first place."

"Do you remember everything about me?"

"Yeah, I do."

"That's really good, Matt," I say, "because I don't think I'm pretty sure I'm falling in love with you. I'm *positive* that I'm crazy in love with you. Have been for a long time."

"You gonna tell your best friend that?" he asks, waggling his eyebrows at me, teasing.

"Are you mad at me for not telling her?" I ask desperately.

He gently touches my face. "That all depends on why you didn't tell her."

"She was upset about Nicholas leaving and her still not knowing if she'd get transferred. I wanted to tell her. I was dying to tell her. But then—" I almost slip and tell him she's pregnant.

"You didn't want to rub your happiness in her face?"

I sigh with relief. "Yes. Exactly. Thank you so much for understanding."

"*Understanding* what?" Hayley says, interrupting us, her arms crossed in front of her and looking like she's not happy with me. Which means she only heard the last thing we said.

"Understanding this," I tell her. Then, I can't help it; I lean in and give Santa a great big kiss, which causes her to screech in shock.

Her eyes are big when I turn to her, still in Matt's arms.

"Did I just get you two together?" she asks.

"Not exactly."

"Not exactly?! Kitty, so help me. If you can't see—"

Matt kisses my forehead and whispers, "I think I'll let you handle this on your own."

Hayley marches over and takes his place in front of me. Then, she shivers and runs her hands down her arms, which are exposed in her holiday party dress. She pulls me back into the house and into one of the bedrooms for privacy.

"What haven't you told me?" she demands.

"Matt and I slept together the night of the wedding."

"What?! Oh my God! Why didn't you tell me at brunch? How did it happen?" She sits on the bed. "And was it good?" She pats a spot beside her and orders me to sit.

I do as I was told, pulling my legs up in a pretzel and facing her. "I've been dying to tell you. But when we were at brunch, you needed to talk about your situation with Nicholas. And then you had the other news. And I wanted to support you, not gush about my new, fantastic sex life and the fact that Matt told me he loves me."

She pulls me into a hug. "There's something I didn't tell you," she whispers.

"Besides that you set me up?"

"No. That wasn't all I was worried about. I was worried about you, dating all these men. I know it sounds like this amazing fantasy, but it's not for you. It's been hard on you. You've had your heart broken. And I wanted to know, if I decided to move, that you'd be okay without me." Tears fill her eyes.

"I'll be okay. I'll be happy for you. I am happy for you."

"And you'll make Matt take you out for nachos and brunches?"

"I promise."

"Then, everything will be okay, and I can go."

"You were thinking of not leaving because of me?" Tears pour out of my eyes.

She nods.

"You really are my best friend."

I see Matt and Nicholas peeking around the door.

"Everything all right in here?" Nicholas asks.

"That all depends," Hayley says, "on how you feel about babies."

"Uh," Nicholas says, "I love babies. Kitty, are you pregnant or something?"

Matt's eyes get huge, but a smile crosses his face. Then, he looks puzzled, wondering if I could be pregnant already. And when he looks up to the ceiling, I can tell he's doing some quick math.

"No," Hayley says. "I am."

Nicholas stands there, frozen for a second, just staring at her. No expression on his face.

Hayley opens her mouth to say something when he rushes toward her, picks her up off her feet, swings her around, and kisses her. "That is the most amazing news I've ever heard."

And that is the most amazing answer I've ever heard.

Matt takes my hand and leads me out of the room, so they can have a little privacy.

WE DON'T SAY much on the ride back to our place. I think we're both still a little overwhelmed by what just happened. The love we witnessed. Or maybe it's because of the fact that, for a moment, Matt thought I was pregnant.

He takes off the suit and tells me he's going to let Phoebe out real quick and that I should open a bottle of wine. I do and even pull out some snacks to go along with it.

When he walks back through the door, I can't help but notice how good he looks. Like irresistible levels of good. It's not like I didn't know he was hot. I've known that since the first time I saw him out in the hallway, back before I ever got up the nerve to say hello. He's certifiably hot. With a hundred percent likelihood of setting a girl's panties on fire.

Now, it's like that but times a million. Like the difference between regular TV and high def. The littlest things catch my attention and basically hypnotize me. Right now, it's the waistband of his shorts peeking out over the top of the sweatpants he threw on. I can't stop staring.

I give Phoebe a doggy cookie, and Matt lights the fire. Still no talking. Which makes me a little nervous. I take the food and drinks over to the coffee table and set everything down on it.

"Admit it," I say to him when he gets the fire going and sits down next to me. "You were a little freaked out when Zack asked me if I was pregnant."

"I was doing the math," he says. "I realized that I don't quite understand the math."

"Well, a woman has her period. The first day of her period is the start of her cycle, which usually runs about twenty-eight days. Some magical time, usually in the middle of those days, she ovulates, and if she has sex during that time and the little swimmer sperm do their thing, she might get pregnant. If she misses her period fourteen or so days later, she can take a test."

"So, you could be pregnant now too? We haven't been super careful with protection. And that's not like me."

"Because you love me and want to put a baby in me?" I tease.

"Honestly, probably unconsciously, yes."

I lean back. Shocked by his words. "Really? I was just joking."

"I'm not. I want to have kids. Do you?"

"I do. Very much so. But if I'm going to have them, I want more than one. It kind of sucked, being an only child. Especially after my parents died."

He picks my wineglass off the table and hands it to me. "Then, a toast," he says. "To us making babies."

What he says is so sweet, I drink to it. Because it is what I want. I just don't know if I want it quite this second. We just finally got together. I want to enjoy us. A lot. For a while.

He wraps his arm around my shoulders, and we lean back into the couch, both quiet, staring at the fire.

I curl up next to him and fall blissfully asleep.

I WAKE UP later to Matt carrying me to my bed.

"Are you leaving?" I ask.

"No, I'm putting us to bed."

"I like that," I murmur as I kiss his neck. "I like being in bed with you."

"I like being in bed with you too."

And he proves it.

Chapter Eight

BUT THE NEXT morning, I wake up alone.

And it gets me thinking. When I write a story, I always give it a big, fat, happy ending. Usually going for the *happily ever after part*, where you know that they will be together forever. My hero and heroine decide they're going to work through their differences or whatever it was that threatened to keep them apart. They realize their love is stronger and more important than any of the outside business going on in their lives—which I will admit, now that I think about it, reminds me of Hayley and Nicholas.

But then what?

I've never really given much thought to what happens after. I haven't had to.

And they certainly didn't lie in bed, like I'm doing now, and think about how all this would work. Like, the logistics of it.

A glance at the clock tells me it's barely eight o'clock.

And I wonder why the man I love isn't here.

I get up, brush my teeth and hair, pull my hair

up into a messy bun, and slip into a silky robe.

Matt's not in my apartment, and neither is Phoebe, so I go across the hall and open his door.

He must not hear me because he doesn't even look up from his computer. He's sitting on the couch, feet up, Phoebe snoring at his side. He's wearing nothing but a pair of sweats. His brown hair is standing almost on end.

"Hey," I say softly, not wanting to wake Phoebe.

"Sorry," he says. "I had to check the news."

"On Sunday morning?"

He glances away from his screen. "Every morning. I have to stay on top of how the market might fluctuate based on news reports. That's why people trust me with their money. They know how thorough I am. You know that about me."

"Sure I do."

Phoebe wakes up and rushes toward me with a toy. I take it from her and toss it down the hall. She darts after it—actually, it's more like she scrambles over the hardwood, legs moving in all directions.

"You sound disappointed."

Though that doesn't get him to turn away from the laptop for good. He's still reading something.

"No, not disappointed."

"So, why do you sound like you are?"

He finally turns my way and gives me his full attention. At least until Phoebe crashes into him. He smiles at her and throws the ball again.

"I guess I wish you had told me you were leaving, is all."

"I didn't want to wake you."

"Oh. Okay." I wrap my arms around myself and slowly back away, toward the door.

I wish I had never come over. I feel stupid for doing this even though I know there's nothing to feel stupid about. I woke up and my—oh, jeez, what is he? My boyfriend? My love?—well, he wasn't there. And I possibly freaked out a little. It's weird, us living so close but not together.

"I didn't want to wake you because today is your big day, and I figured you'd want to be well rested. And, well, I didn't really let you rest last night. Do you want breakfast?" Matt asks. "I could make something."

First off, now, I feel bad for the way I acted. I also totally forgot that today is the day I've been dreading.

I shake my head. "Oh crap. I forgot about it. I think Lois said the crew is coming over around ten, so I'd better hurry up, take a shower, and get ready."

"You want me to come over and hang out while it's happening? I don't have anyplace else to be."

"Honestly, I'd probably only be more nervous if you were there."

"Got it." He narrows his eyes. "Are you sure you're okay?"

"Yep. Just fine. Nervous."

"Don't be." He comes to me and takes my face

in his hands, and things feel okay again.

"You know how worried I am about the interview."

He strokes my cheeks with his thumbs, leaning down until our noses nearly touch. "I know, but you'll get through it, and you'll completely kill it. And when it's over, you'll feel a hundred times better, knowing you were brave enough to do this."

"Thank you for being here for me." I cover his hands with mine, looking up into his eyes. "Always. You've always been here. Even when we were fighting or generally annoyed with each other, I could always count on you."

"And you still can. Forever." He wraps me in his arms and holds me close while Phoebe runs in circles around us.

I guess we don't need to figure out everything all at once. We can take our time. Right now, this is enough.

Chapter Nine

"NOW, ALL YOU have to do is look pretty and smile for the camera. You can do that, right?"

Lois hovers over me, tucking a piece of hair behind my ear, which the hairstylist only moves again. I'm surprised she doesn't swat my agent's hand away, but then Lois is an older lady. One doesn't swat away an older lady even if that hand is threatening to undo a lot of very careful work.

"Something tells me I'll be doing a little more than smiling." I sit up as straight and tall as I can, hands folded in my lap. There's a soft blue backdrop behind me and a ring light positioned in front of me, behind the camera, which will beam my face to however many thousands or even millions of people who will eventually watch this interview.

Good Lord. So many people. Watching me, listening to me.

There's a reason writers sit behind computers and don't have to watch people reading and reacting to their stories. There's a reason we have the opportunity to polish our words, to write and rewrite them until they shine.

"She's sweating again," the makeup girl says.

Surely, I'm not her first nervous client.

"Sorry," I whisper to her.

She applies more powder at my hairline before backing away.

Now, I wish I hadn't told Matt I could handle this on my own.

"I could offer a little extra confidence," he reminded me just before I left his apartment to get ready for the hair and makeup people.

I still turned him down though since it felt like this was something I should handle on my own.

I know it was the right decision. No matter how supportive he wants to be, it would only make me more nervous to have him here. I would rather get this over with in front of as few people I know personally as possible. Not even Hayley's presence would calm my nerves.

"Kitty? Can you hear me?" The voice in my earpiece makes me jump, but I smile for the camera anyway.

That's maybe the most unnerving part about all of this. I'll be talking to a camera, not an actual person. I'll only hear the voice of my interviewer, Hugh Pearson, through the earpiece. I could be anywhere in the entire world, but I have to pretend that I can see him. That I'm talking to him.

How do people do this all the time?

"I can hear you," I assure him.

And now, I am kicking myself for not looking

up a photo of him, so I could put a face to the voice and imagine that he was actually here.

And then I realize that's exactly what I do when I'm writing. I imagine. And I have a good imagination. So, I look at the camera and pretend to see a face. The handsome face of an older man. A man like Peter. Yes, Peter is kind. He's sweet. He makes me feel comfortable.

I can do this. I can.

"Okay, Kitty, we have thirty seconds. Just relax. Don't overthink it."

It's like he's reading my mind.

"Just pretend we're two friends sitting in your living room, talking about your career."

"If we were friends, wouldn't you already know about my career?" I ask.

"Huh?"

"Forget it." *Wow, I'm already off to a great start.* Maybe it's better for me to get all that awkward nonsense out of the way before the interview officially goes live.

"I don't know that she's meant for on-camera interviews," Lois says.

Why she has to be here, I have no idea.

Hugh pipes up again, "Okay, Kitty, we're going to lead in. Take a deep breath and relax, and it will all be over before you know it."

Isn't that the sort of thing doctors say to patients before they're about to have a procedure done? I have to bite my tongue to stay quiet and press my folded hands between my thighs to keep them from shaking. Besides, I don't know what to do with them. I tend to talk with my hands, and something tells me that won't go over well during an interview where I'm supposed to be very sophisticated, worldly, and intelligent.

My readers have no idea what they're in for.

"Bookworms, I'm Hugh Pearson, and I have a treat for you. I'm here with *New York Times* best-selling author Kitty Valentine."

I smile big with my teeth clenched.

"Relax," Lois whispers from somewhere behind the camera.

I can't really see her with the ring light in my eyes, but I take her advice and loosen my jaw slightly. Now, I might actually be able to talk—with the added bonus of getting through this without cracking any teeth.

What I imagine is Hugh's cheesy smile shines through in his voice.

No, picture Peter. Sweet Peter.

"Kitty, thank you for taking time out of your busy writing schedule to talk with us today."

"Thank you for the opportunity." That sounded almost normal, didn't it? "Sometimes, it's nice speaking to another person instead of making up conversations in my head."

Note to self: quit while you're ahead. It's like I can't make myself stop talking.

At least I don't have to look at what I can only

imagine is a blank expression from the man doing the interview.

He recovers quickly. "So, tell me a little bit about this unconventional arrangement that you and your publisher came up with."

Yes, because I have to pretend it was all my publisher's idea. At the end of the day, they have to be the big hero. "They wanted me to add more heat to my books, and it was suggested that I gain a little real-world experience by choosing the most popular tropes in romance and dating men who aligned with those tropes."

"And can you explain that to me? The concept of a trope?"

We've been through the questions already, so I'm not speaking completely off the cuff now. Knowing at least most of what I'm going to say keeps my pulse from racing too far out of control and helps my voice stay even.

"If you take a look at my list of most recently published books, you'll see what I mean. There are a number of popular characters in romance nowadays, the sort of characters readers expect to see. A firefighter, a doctor, an athlete. It's the same with movies—the lonesome cowboy, the hard-working cub reporter, looking to make a name for himself. We went for the most popular, most in-demand types of characters, and I set out on finding real-life inspiration. For research purposes."

"So, you have a few more notches in your headboard now, is that it?"

My smile slips. Actually, it drops off my face with a resounding thud. This was most definitely not on the list of questions, and I can feel my face starting to heat up. "Not necessarily," I manage to say. "There's something to be said for fiction and a writer's imagination."

"Come on. You mean to tell me that you didn't take any of your book's steamier scenes from real life? I have an excerpt from one of them here, if you don't mind me reading it out loud."

I can hear Lois muttering something behind the ring light. I don't have to make out her exact words to know she's not happy with the way this is going. They must've given her an earpiece too. But she's not wearing a microphone the way I am, which is probably for the best. They would have to bleep out some—*most all*—of the words she's saying.

A nervous, choked little laugh escapes me while I stare blankly into the camera and wish I could strangle the sneaky, awful man conducting the interview. "Honestly, I don't know—"

Too late. "*He lowered his head between her thighs and …*"

He goes on, and I want to slide off my chair and keep going until I sink straight into the ground. I'm blushing—I know I am—and I can only imagine how it must look for the people watching. Like I'm so embarrassed by my own work that I can't bear to hear it read out loud.

It's easier just to sit here and let it happen without arguing. I manage to keep a smile on my face as the interviewer reads a few more lines. He has to stop eventually since things heat up substantially, because there's got to be a limit to what he's allowed to say.

He chuckles on finishing. "Whew! You mean to tell me that didn't happen in real life? You had to make that all up in your head?"

"Writers have been making up situations like that and many others in their heads for a very long time," I point out. "For as long as the romance genre has existed in fact. I doubt every single author draws their work from real life. Otherwise, how would they have any time to get work done?"

I can hear somebody snorting somewhere in the room. It gives me courage to keep going. "I hate to burst your bubble, Hugh, but the life of a romance author isn't lived between the sheets. I spend most of my days in front of my laptop, trying to make sense of the words coming out of my head."

"You mean to say you've never had any fun during *any* of your dates?"

"Oh, sure, there's fun, but then there's the sort of fun you were just talking about. I enjoyed dating every single one of the men who inspired my work. All of them brought something different to my life, and they inevitably taught me about myself. I feel like I've grown as a person and as a writer, thanks to them."

"What do you think about the news that just broke regarding one of your past subjects?"

"I … don't quite know what you're talking about."

"So, you aren't aware of allegations by Dustin Grant, who claims you promised compensation for the use of his likeness in your book?"

That jerk. This is the first I'm hearing of it, but I believe it. It's just the kind of thing he would do. "It's news to me, I can honestly say."

"Would you like to let your side of the story be heard here and now?"

There's like, and then there's *like.*

Yes, I would very much like to let my side of the story be heard here and now. I would very much like to tell the world about good old Dustin, who figured I would reinvigorate his career. He wanted to use me, nothing more than that. The loser.

Then again, something tells me neither Maggie nor her bosses would like it, no matter how much my interviewer would. Something tells me *he* would like it a whole lot. Because it would make for a juicy story—no pun intended.

I can see Lois waving her hands back and forth. She doesn't want me to say a word. And I'm not about to.

"I don't feel at liberty to speak on it right now, and I think it would be better for my publisher to do the talking."

Is he going to argue with me? Will he press the sub-

ject?

Thankfully, no.

Or so I think.

"Maybe you have something to say to Dustin then. Dustin? Are you on with us?"

I don't care that I'm live and everybody can see me. I look over the camera to where Lois is frantically punching numbers into her phone.

"Actually, no, Hugh, I have nothing to say to Dustin."

"Kitty, let's not be that way," Dustin says. "We had a lot of fun when we were together. I only want my share of the book's profits. That's all I've ever wanted."

Oh, he makes my blood boil over, but I can't look that way on camera.

"What do you think, Kitty?" Hugh says. "Does Dustin deserve a cut of your royalties since you took so much of the book based on your relationship from real life?"

I can't sit here and not say anything, can I? Who would put up with this and not say a single word? My head's spinning, thoughts colliding, and the tiny part of me that's still operating from good sense is dwindling to the size of a pinprick in the face of cold, hard disgust.

In other words, I want to tear this jerk a new one.

Instead, I lift my chin and resolve to be as dignified as possible. I might not always say or do the right thing, but I can be dignified when I have to. *Thank you, Grandmother.*

"We discussed this at the time we parted—and I wouldn't call what we had a relationship. We dated casually for a little while. I changed nearly all of the facts and circumstances for the sake of keeping it fictional. I don't think anyone who read the book ever imagined I was writing about Dustin Grant. Because I wasn't."

"That's what you think. I can't tell you how many people pointed out the similarities between the main character and me," Dustin argues.

I'm sure he can't tell me because it never actually happened. *Good Lord, how did I ever feel he was worth the time of day? What was I thinking?*

Hugh is loving this. I don't have to see him to know he is. "What do you say to that, Kitty?"

My mouth opens, but Lois makes a strangled noise before I can tell both men just exactly what I have to say to that. Good thing since what is on the tip of my tongue is most certainly not viewer friendly and might get me fired.

"I say, speak with my publisher, as I'm sure they'll be better suited to have this conversation than me."

I hear Dustin snort while Hugh sighs, but he accepts what I said. "Fair enough. One question: who are you dating this time? Who can we expect to see in your next book?"

God, this is so fake. I feel like the biggest phony

in the entire world, like an idiot, even while my skin crawls and sweat runs down the back of my neck.

"You'll just have to wait for the book to come out, same as everybody else." *Do I sound a little snippy? Probably, and I don't care.*

It's such a relief when the interview ends, and I can't wait to tear the earpiece out of my ear and the microphone from the collar of my shirt.

"What was that about?" I ask Lois, who's already getting on her phone.

"I don't know, doll, but I'm about to get to the bottom of it. Open a window, get some fresh air. You look like you could use some."

I could use more than fresh air. I could use a drink, maybe two, and a certain has-been musician's head on a stick.

Chapter Ten

"WHAT A DISASTER," I groan, dramatically tossing myself across Matt's couch and telling him what just happened.

"I'm sure it's not that bad," he says.

I raise my hand from across my eyes and shoot him a look. "Really? Because I heard he's doing an interview for some online tabloid next."

"Let him do all the interviews he wants. Something tells me he's going to end up shooting himself in the foot."

"What makes you say that?" I ask.

"For one thing, you never used his name in the book."

"That's true."

"So, right there, he's going to make himself look like an idiot for jumping on your coattails and trying to steal a little of your fifteen minutes of fame."

"You think it will only be fifteen minutes?"

He groans with a gentle snicker at the end. "That would be the part you latched on to, wouldn't it?"

I nudge him with my foot, which happens to currently be in his lap. "Okay, so let's say he comes out and complains more that I wrote about him. Or he says I made things up to make him look bad."

"But you didn't."

"I can think of a couple of things that happened in the book that he could say I tore from real life to make him look bad. I wish I had never met him." I cover my face with my hands again. "And to think, I was so excited about it at the time."

"You were pretty excited, weren't you?" His voice goes high-pitched. *Oh, I get to date my first big crush! I get to live out my childhood dreams! If only the mean girls I went to school with could see me now!*"

"Please. And I'm sure you wouldn't be thrilled to meet a girl you had a crush on when you were a kid."

"I was more into worshipping my favorite athletes. Hockey players, football players, baseball players. Now, that would be cool to meet some of them."

"What if they turned out to be jerks who would step on your neck if it meant getting themselves ahead?"

"I don't think I'd be too surprised."

"That's because you're such a cynic," I say.

"Sometimes, that's what happens to a person when they get kicked in the teeth one too many times."

I nudge him again, but this time, it's to make

him look at me. "I'll never kick you in the teeth."

"That makes me feel so much better."

"I mean, I've wanted to in the past," I say, a smile crossing my face and making me feel better.

"That comes as no surprise."

"Tell the truth. There were times when you *wanted* to get on my nerves."

"Please, I lived to get on your nerves for a while there. I wanted to get your attention any way I could."

"I thought so."

"Don't let this go to your head, but you're pretty cute when you're fired up."

"I feel like that's supposed to be a compliment, but I don't feel super great about it."

He laughs. "You should."

"And you should see a doctor about the size of your ego."

"You're probably right about that too."

He goes back to rubbing my feet, which is what he was doing when we started this conversation. If it wasn't for him, I would be halfway through a bottle of vodka by now.

"So, you think this is going to be okay?" I ask, afraid to hope.

"I think it's going to be better than okay. I think this is going to be one of those things that flares up out of nowhere and then goes away. The guy is a loser. Always has been. The public is going to take this for what it is: a last-ditch effort at getting his name out there. A pathetic jerk trying to cling to the last scraps of fame. I guess you know by now that his comeback tour fizzled out."

"I have to say, I wasn't paying attention." That was a deliberate move on my part. I didn't want to hear or read his name ever again. Knowing he got drunk enough to fall off the party boat rented by Hayley's firm made me laugh pretty hard, but that was as far as I was willing to go.

"Let's just say, I kept my eye out for mentions of his name." When I raise an eyebrow, he sighs. "Okay, so I had a Google Alert set for his name. Sue me."

"That's actually very sweet."

"You think so? Because I didn't exactly have very sweet things in mind when I did it." He might be rubbing a little harder than he needs to, but I know it's only a reflection of what's going on in his head. Nothing nice or pleasant, and it's all because of me. For my sake.

"You know … we have a lot of things to talk about." I keep my voice even, light.

"We do."

"So … should we start talking?" I ask.

"I thought we were talking already."

"You being a smart-ass makes me want to kill you. Still. You know that, right?"

"I do."

"And now that we've kissed in front of a bunch of witnesses, they'll believe I would never do such a thing to you. We're in love and everything. So, that's my defense."

"It's obvious you write romance and not mystery or thriller books. The significant other is *always* the first person the cops look at. Watch a true crime show."

"Shut up."

"Anyway, you want to talk about us. Is that where this is going? You wanna know what happens next?"

"Um, yeah. Don't you?"

"Sure, I guess."

"You guess?" I sit up straight and take my feet back, tucking them under me.

"No, don't do that."

"Don't do what?"

"Don't pull back just because I'm not giving you the answer you want to hear. The fact is, I don't know what happens next. Isn't it enough to let things unfold the way they're supposed to unfold?"

"No!"

He bursts out laughing. "Then, I don't know what to tell you. You can't be in control of everything. That's not how life works."

I sigh.

"But I do have a few ideas, Valentine," he says with a grin.

"What kind of ideas, Ryder? Because I hate waking up and not having you there."

"Well, we do have very different schedules. I

don't expect you to change yours because of me."

"Will you run off after we have sex though? That's what I want to know. I don't like waking up alone with no warning."

He slides over on the couch and pulls me into his arms. "No, I won't run off after we have sex. And I haven't. I let you sleep. And you knew exactly where I was."

"Are we going to keep both apartments?" I blurt out.

"Uh …" He sounds surprised, maybe a little taken aback.

"I don't think it's a bad question." I push away from his chest and look at him.

"I like my space."

"Doesn't it seem silly for us to be together and still have separate apartments that are next door to each other? Like wasteful almost?"

His frown makes my heart hurt.

"You're talking about moving in together," he says slowly.

"Yes. Combining our living spaces and saving ourselves a mortgage payment by getting rid of one of the apartments."

"But with our schedules being so different, doesn't it make more sense for us to have our own space? For when it's four thirty and you're only just wrapping up your work for the night while I'm on my way out for a run after sleeping for several hours?"

"I guess so."

"And when you're sleeping and I'm working? Or when I'm sleeping and you're cursing out the character who won't tell you what to have them do next?"

"I don't do that."

"You've done it. I've heard you."

"Okay. Maybe once, but that's it."

"You get my point." He's laughing as he pulls me in for another hug. "Let me think about it, okay?"

Maybe I'm overthinking this. Wouldn't be the first time, won't be the last, but I'm a little hurt by his response. In a book, he would wrap his arms around me, swing me through the air in happiness, kiss me, and tell me living together would make him the happiest man in the world. Like what Nicholas did for Hayley the other day.

"Yeah. Sure," I say, trying not to sound disappointed.

He kisses the tip of my nose. "Good."

Chapter Eleven

"I BASICALLY FELT like a total idiot. The man had a complete deer-in-headlights look, and I was sure he was going to tell me this was all a mistake. That we're not meant to last. I mean, who wants a girlfriend who's always pushing just a little too hard?"

"You didn't push too hard. You asked completely normal questions. I envy you."

I wince at the sad note in Hayley's voice. "I shouldn't even be talking to you about this."

"Nonsense. I'm still your best friend. This is what I do."

"Yeah, but—"

"No buts. You don't have to avoid talking about the biggest thing in your life just because Nicholas is gone." Her voice cracks a little on that last word. I figure it's my duty as her best friend to pretend like I didn't hear it.

I know her. I know the more I insist she talk about it, the worse she'll feel. She'll get mad at me for pushing and even more upset over missing her man, which will make her angrier until she bursts out crying at work.

Granted, I called her in the middle of the morning to check in and make sure she was okay, but that doesn't mean I have to add insult to injury. I only indulged her by answering her Matt questions because it was obvious she wanted to talk about something else.

I won't bother asking about her transfer. Or what she and Nicholas decided to do about her job and living arrangements. If she wants to tell me, she will.

"Where are you right now?" she asks as I walk into a home store a few blocks from my place.

"I'm just out, wandering around. Shopping. Trying to cheer myself up after the disaster that was my interview, followed by the disaster that was my conversation with Matt."

"You shouldn't worry about that. Dustin was an ass. I can't believe I ever crushed on him."

"Yeah, me neither. I'm thinking a new rug for my kitchen and some candles."

"Oh, candles always make me feel better. And wine—except now … no wine."

"Do you want to talk about all that?"

"Not right now. I'm still processing. We're still processing."

"He had an amazing reaction though. Seriously, Hayley. It was the kind of scene I could have written in one of my books."

"He did. It made me feel good. Really good."

"I think that's kind of why I'm bummed about Matt."

"Because you didn't get the reaction you wanted? You shouldn't be, Kitty. You can't control everything. And I should know. I've tried to."

"But I shouldn't be bummed?" I ask, stopping to smell a pink grapefruit candle.

"No, I'm changed. I'm going to let fate decide. Wait to see if I get the transfer before freaking out. Once I know, then I'll deal with it. Scratch that. *We'll* deal with it."

"Good plan. I'm actually going to do the same, believe it or not. If and when Matt wants us to move in together, he can let me know. I will not speak of it again."

I pick up another candle and smell it. "What do you think? Pink Grapefruit for a fresh, clean scent, or should I go full-on holiday spirit with Cinnamon Pine?"

"Pine," she says.

I drop it in the little basket I picked up by the door.

"Excuse me. Aren't you that writer?"

I turn at the sound of a voice just over my shoulder. It makes me jump a little too, as I didn't notice a person standing so close to me.

"Everything okay?" Hayley asks.

I hold up a finger to the girl standing with me—she's young, maybe in her late teens—and tell Hayley I'll call her back.

I turn to the girl. "Sorry. You were asking if I'm a writer?"

Her head bobs up and down. "Yeah. I saw you on Hugh Pearson's show. I thought it was bullshit, the way he put you on the spot."

"That's nice of you to say." I mean, sort of. Not the way she said it, but the sentiment behind it.

Then, I notice a second girl standing halfway down the aisle with her phone held out in front of her. She's recording this along with a couple of friends who are wearing wide smiles.

"Um, sorry, but could you not do that?" I ask them as gently as I can.

The girl looks up at me from her phone screen. "It's just to post on my feed. No big deal."

"I would rather you didn't, please." I can't believe this.

I want to hold my hand in front of my face to hide myself, though it occurs to me that I haven't done anything to warrant hiding. I haven't done anything wrong. I'm shopping for candles, for goodness' sake.

"It's publicity for you. You deserve to be heard, Kitty."

Where do they even get off, calling me by my first name like we're friends? I don't know them, and I don't want them knowing my personal business.

But it's too late for that, isn't it? Just like my dad used to say, *"You can't put the toothpaste back in the* tube."

I've been trying to ignore the publicity stuff. I haven't checked in on what Dustin has been saying about me, about our relationship. It's easier to ignore it for the sake of my sanity—not to mention, my blood pressure. I'm too young to have a stroke over this, and Dustin isn't worth it.

Looks like there's only so much I can ignore.

"What's happening here?" One of the store employees finds us and looks concerned when she sizes up what's going on.

Then, something changes in her expression. Her eyes widen a little. "Oh, it's you! I saw something about you on TV this morning. There was a story about that musician—"

"Please. I don't want to talk about that." I try to elbow my way past the girl as gently as I can, knowing I'm being recorded the whole time. "Just let me by, please."

"Wait! Don't you want to tell your side of the story?" The girl with the camera is following me down the aisle, right on my heels.

Now, there are a few more people watching, closing in.

Do they know who I am or why this is happening, or are they only curious onlookers?

None of them tries to help me—that's all I know.

"I can't talk about it. Please, leave me alone now. I'm just here to shop." There's a tremor in my voice, and I hate hearing it, but never in my life have I felt so boxed in.

People are asking questions, muttering to each other. A few of them are snickering like this is a joke, like it's an amusement rather than an actual person's actual life.

There's a restroom in the back, and I just about throw myself inside and lock the door.

Now, I can breathe. Now, I can think, even with my name being called out just on the other side of the cold metal.

So, there are millions of people in Manhattan, and I'll never be recognized, huh?

That makes me think about Matt, who I text with shaking fingers. I tell him where I am and what happened. Then follow it with: *Please, come get me. I can't face all these people alone.*

"Kitty, we only want to help you! It's so unfair that you don't get to have your voice heard! What are you trying to hide?"

I close my eyes and barely hold back a whimper.

Whimpering is the last thing I want to do. What I want is to scream at them. To ask who they think they are. What right they have to ask me personal questions, to hound me when I flat-out asked them to leave me alone.

I want to tell them to get lives while I'm at it.

It's not too long before Matt's voice joins the ones outside the restroom. "Okay, okay, back off. Leave her alone now. She has nothing to say to you." Then, close to the door, he says, "It's me.

Come on out."

I keep my head down and let Matt put an arm around me, holding me close to his side and ushering me through the crowd. There must be twenty people.

What, did they call their friends to join them?

"Enough. Move out of the way. Let us through." He looks down at the basket I'm still carrying. "I think we can leave this here."

I forgot all about it. He takes it from me and leaves it by the door before we're outside.

"YOU OKAY?" MATT hands me a cup of tea and perches on the coffee table in front of where I'm currently curled up on the couch.

"I overreacted. I freaked out."

"There were about two dozen people crowded around that damn restroom door. What were you supposed to do? They didn't even back off when I asked them to. You'd think we were a pair of criminals, the way they followed us through the store." He strokes my leg with a frown. "I hate to think of you going through that alone."

"I didn't have to though, did I?" I offer what I hope passes for a smile. "You came to my rescue."

"I'll always be around to rescue you. I promise."

"Good, because it seems like I need a lot of rescuing."

He winks, smirking. "Not like I didn't already know that."

"It would be a day without sunshine, wouldn't it? If you ever missed an opportunity to smirk over something about me?"

"Probably, yeah."

I wish I could joke around and be lighthearted, but I'm still shaken up. I can't think of anything but all those people asking questions and wanting to record me for social media. What's wrong with them?

"Can I ask you something?"

Matt nods at me in response.

"Good. Do you still have that Google Alert set up for Dustin's name?"

When he growls, I know the answer is yes. Not like I thought he wasn't keeping tabs, but I thought it made sense to ask.

"So, it's true about him giving interviews, huh?"

"Honestly, I'm surprised you haven't been hounded a lot worse than what just happened earlier. I didn't want to say anything about it. I can only imagine Lois and Maggie are both fielding a lot of phone calls right now. Interview requests and all that."

"So I can tell my side of the story." I roll my eyes and sink back against the cushions with a sigh. "It's so stupid. I'm nobody important."

"That's not true."

"But I'm not. I've lived in this city my whole life. I'm not one of those famous people."

"You are now. Maybe not a huge celebrity like a

movie star, but you're a public personality. It'll die down. We'll ride this out."

We. We'll ride this out.

Matt's face falls when tears fill my eyes, blurring him a little. I can tell he's upset though.

"No, no, don't cry. You'll be okay. This isn't forever."

I only shake my head, laughing a little at myself now. Boy, he must think I'm a human roller coaster with all these ups and downs. Then again, he knows me.

"These aren't sad tears. I'm touched. It means so much to hear you say that."

"It's the truth. You and me, right?"

When he says it like that and holds my hand, I can't help but believe him. Good thing, too, because I really want to.

Chapter Twelve

"AND HERE WE are in Sicily. We ate the most incredible fresh seafood there." My grandmother closes her eyes with a faint, satisfied smile. "It came directly from the sea. I've never been so impressed."

"It looks pretty … simple." I don't know a better way to say what immediately comes to mind when I look through these pictures from Grandmother's honeymoon.

"You mean, it looks like something I would never do. Be honest."

I glance up at her from the stack of photos—honestly, it's cute, the fact that she had actual photos printed—with a wince. "Sorry. I have a hard time imagining you in a rented house, eating seaside at a shack of a restaurant."

"Life is more than The Plaza, dear."

"Tell me you didn't sometimes wish you were traveling a little fancier."

She sighs. "Once or twice. But honestly, we had the richest, most wonderful experiences. Dancing until the wee hours of the morning in Barcelona. Eating gelato on the Spanish Steps. We took our time, rested whenever we wished, dined fabulously, and met so many lovely people. I can't wait to get back."

"Where?"

"Everywhere, all of it."

She's definitely my grandmother. I would've said the same thing. Why choose only one when everything is amazing?

Peter's chuckling when he joins us. "Don't let this one fool you with this talk of resting. She walked my feet off."

"I don't recall hearing you complain."

The smile they share makes my heart swell. They're the sweetest thing. After the last few days since being rescued by Matt at the store, I need something to take my mind off my troubles.

Sure, having him by my side is an incredible gift, but even he can't make everything better. He doesn't own a magic wand. Lois called three times this morning alone to update me on yet another series of interviews, all of which will be on camera.

Because the first one went so well.

Once she's finished making eyes at her new husband, she turns back to me. "You look tired. Have you been taking care of yourself?"

"Things have been sort of wild lately. You've missed a lot."

"Such as?"

The two of them wait patiently, looking at me with expectant expressions.

So, it looks like I have to tell all.

By the time I give them the blow-by-blow on the interviews and the incident at the store, my grandmother's cheeks are bright red. Not from rouge either.

"How dare that filthy, disgusting piece of—"

"Now, now." Peter takes her hand. "Remember your heart."

"My heart? What about my granddaughter? What about so-called journalists possessing a scrap of integrity? How dare anyone put you on the spot that way!"

Now, I'm starting to get concerned too. "I shouldn't have mentioned it. I should've known how it would upset you."

"Upset me? You're concerned about me when you were forced to hide in a public restroom, thanks to this? When you cannot so much as walk down the street to run an errand without being bombarded?"

"Cecile." Peter's voice is firmer this time. "I'm going to have to ask you to control yourself better. I realize you don't want to listen to anyone telling you what to do, but for your sake, calm down."

"It's okay." I take her hand and rub it, noticing the way the pulse in her wrist races. "Everything will be fine. I have Matt to help me." Then, I slap my forehead. "Duh. I didn't tell you about that either."

"About what?"

I look at her and then at Peter. "Matt and I are ... you know."

"Together?" Peter's brow lifts as he starts to smile. "Really?"

"Oh dear!" Grandmother takes her hands back from the two of us and claps them together. It's like a total about-face. Now, she's beaming, laughing. "It took long enough! How did he finally convince you?"

"You make it sound like I had to be dragged, kicking and screaming."

She pins me with a sly, knowing look. "Didn't you?"

"It wasn't quite that dramatic."

"Perhaps I should let you ladies talk about it privately." Peter starts to get up, but I shake my head.

"You're family. And it's not like I'm going to start sharing dirty details."

"Kathryn!" Grandmother gasps.

"Oh, don't start clutching your pearls now, you."

"She has a point." Peter's smiling with a tender look in his eyes.

Did it mean that much to him to hear me call him family? He is after all. As far as I'm concerned, he's been family for a long time.

Grandmother sighs heavily. "Am I to be forever outnumbered? Is that what this is going to turn into?"

I point to her, looking at Peter. "Is that what I sound like when I sigh?"

"Should I answer truthfully?"

"All right, enough." Grandmother makes a slashing motion in the air with her hand. "I need to know when the wedding will be held. We have so much work to do."

My mouth falls open. Even Peter looks surprised.

Finally, I'm able to speak, though it comes out as a strained croak. "Who said anything about a wedding?"

"Who needs to?" She lifts a shoulder. "It's obvious the two of you are meant to be married and to live ... how do you put it in your books? Happily ever after?"

"Well, I don't know that I write those actual words."

"No, but you lead the readers to believe they will have that. Regardless, you are ignoring my point. The two of you will obviously be wed. I've seen it all along."

"Has Matt hinted of matrimony yet?" Peter asks with a grin. "You have known each other for quite some time. No reason to wait."

"Are you kidding? I made the vague suggestion that we should share an apartment, and he didn't respond the way I'd expected. I wasn't trying to force him into anything, but he might have taken it that way."

"You were only being reasonable and pragmatic," Grandmother assures me.

"Exactly."

When Peter snorts, I glare at him.

"What?"

He sits back with an overly innocent expression. "Nothing. I know better."

Meanwhile, my grandmother's brain is working overtime. "Spring. A spring wedding would be lovely."

"Would you stop, please?" I have to bury my face in my hands. "I almost wish I'd never told you."

"No, no, I'm relieved you did. Even if it means having to keep my wedding planning quiet, for fear of your reaction." She calms down and gets serious. "I can't tell you how relieved I am to know you aren't alone. You have someone to lean on. I know too well how important that is. Frankly, I'm not certain how I managed without it as long as I did."

"You've had Peter by your side for longer than I've been alive," I point out.

She smiles, turning to him. "That's right. I have."

He kisses her cheek, and I just about die from the cuteness.

My phone buzzes where I left it next to me on my chair. When Grandmother shoots me a disapproving look, I have to defend myself. "I'm waiting on calls from my agent and editor over an interview

I'm supposed to give either tomorrow or the next day. This one is supposed to go better. We'll see."

It's an unknown number though, not one of theirs or anybody's I recognize.

I've been getting a lot of calls from unknown numbers lately. They never leave a voice mail, so I have no way of knowing who's calling. I guess there's nothing overly weird about that.

Though I can't help but wonder whether this is part of everything else going on. I'm not naive. I know how easy it is to find just about anything on the internet. Every cell number ever associated with a person, every address they've ever lived at. The whole nine yards.

Would somebody go so far as to look up my number? If so, why? Well, I've already seen some of the why for myself, in person. At least I can choose not to answer the phone.

"If you don't figure out some way to keep your wedding ideas to yourself over the holidays, I'm not bringing Matt with me to dinner." I shrug with a grimace. "Sorry. That's the way it has to be."

"How can you expect me to agree to that?" She throws her hands into the air. "You mean to say, I can't so much as hint at it?"

I just shake my head and give her a shrug.

LATER, ONCE I'M outside and seriously reconsidering spending the holidays with my grandmother, the phone rings again. Again, it's an unknown number.

Call me crazy. Call me stupid. But I can't stop myself from answering this time as I'm ducking into a car Peter suggested I get to take me home. Normally, I'd walk to the subway, maybe do a little window shopping on the way.

I can't trust the people around me right now, and that's just about the most depressing thing in the world. I can't count on being left alone, and I'm not going to walk around in disguise.

So, I have no choice but to get a hired black car and duck straight into my building afterward. The person calling me right now might well be one of the people responsible for that.

Which is why I bark out a curt, "Hello?" on answering as I walk up the steps.

Instead of sneering or laughing on the other end, there's a smooth female voice. "Mr. Blake Marlin calling for Miss Kitty Valentine."

Which is when I have to juggle the phone after it slips out of my hand and almost hits the floor. "Hold on, hold on, hold on!" I get a better hold on it and put it back against my ear, breathless. "Hello?"

"Are you available to speak to Mr. Marlin?"

"Uh, yes."

Holy mackerel. I never thought Blake would actually call. He's, like, at the very top of the top of the totem pole over at my publisher since he owns the corporation that owns the company.

That basically owns me.

He also happens to be the first man I dated

when I started this wacky project Maggie had come up with.

A moment passes before he gets on the line. "Kitty Valentine. You troublesome little—"

"I can explain, Blake."

"Oh?"

Crap. Now, he expects me to explain. "I didn't have anything to do with all this trouble. It wasn't my idea to start doing interviews. I was against the idea from the very beginning, but I was way outvoted, so there wasn't much I could do about it."

He's quiet for a second. A very, very long second. A second that stretches out for hours.

Or is it just me?

"Are you finished?"

Oh boy, I sure do wish he didn't sound so disappointed. "I think so. Um … it's nice to hear from you, and I hope you're doing well."

He might think I can't hear him snort with laughter, but he'd be wrong. And that's like the pin that pops the balloon. I fall back against my door with my eyes closed, one hand over my chest.

"Kitty, did you honestly think I was calling to yell at you? And what's with it taking so long to answer the damn phone? I've been trying to get ahold of you for days."

"You have?"

"Yes."

"Because you were upset, but the passage of time has soothed your anger a little?"

"I was never angry. Not at you anyway."

"Really? Even with all this drama? What about what Dustin is saying? What about the lies he's telling?"

"You have nothing to worry about."

"I know you're only saying that to make me feel better."

"Actually, I'm not. I'm telling you the truth. There's nothing to worry about."

Does the man live in an alternate universe?

"He's spilling his guts all over the place, saying we did all sorts of things we never did. He's lying!"

"I know that. It'll be okay. I had him sign a non-disclosure agreement—NDA for short—before your book was ever published. The way all of your guys did."

My head snaps back. "Are you serious?"

"As a heart attack. What, did you think I would leave you or my company open to legal complications? Trust me, it's taken care of."

It's all coming at me so fast that I barely know which nugget of information to focus on first. "Wait a second. I never provided you with any real names."

"I realize that."

"Then, how did you know who to go to?"

"Kitty, come on. You're a smart person. Do you think I was born yesterday?"

"No."

"You've seen for yourself the sort of life I live.

The resources at my disposal. When you think about it that way, you should know I would have no problem locating anybody."

The man has a point. He once flew me to a different city on his private jet just to have dinner.

"So, you tracked them all down?"

"Not me personally, no. I have people who do that for me." He chuckles when I gasp in surprise. "Hey, aren't you the one who was always trying to get me to loosen up and let other people handle some of the responsibility?"

"So, you got them all to sign an agreement not to say anything?"

"Of course! How could I not? As soon as I knew this was what you were going to be doing after you and I stopped seeing each other and when I saw how much of my personal life you were exposed to, there was no other choice. I had to make sure the rest of the guys who came after me would keep their mouths shut."

"So, I really don't have to worry about him?"

"That's what I've been trying to tell you. Dustin signed the NDA, and so did his manager. And when I tell you it was airtight, you can believe me. My lawyers don't leave anything to chance."

That much I can believe. "He's been blabbing all over the place though. True things, lies, all sorts of stuff."

"He probably figures he can get plenty for talking through interviews and such, that the publicity will be enough to boost his record sales. So, what's a little old lawsuit in the face of that?" He snorts. "He'll find out. I've been biding my time, giving him enough rope to hang himself with. I hope he sleeps well tonight since it'll be the last opportunity he has to do so for quite a while."

"I don't know what to say."

"Well, don't take this the wrong way, but I didn't do it for you. I did it for the publisher. It's just part of doing business. Knowing I was covering your ass was gravy."

"Even though you didn't do it for me, thank you. You went out of your way to get in touch with me, and that means a lot. I know what a busy guy you are."

"I've been trying to be a little less busy lately. That was your influence, by the way. I know I said I arranged for the agreements to cover my ass, but that's not completely true. I wanted to make sure you were safe too. You're a special person, and I was sorry for a long time that we couldn't make things work. The least I could do was protect you from guys like this, who only want to cash in on your talent and ability."

"I don't know what to say. I'm flattered. Deeply touched."

"But I have to ask you something."

"Should I be nervous?"

He laughs. "When are you going to settle down? Are you ever going to get tired of bouncing from one man to another?"

"You tell me, boss. I'm doing this for your publishing company."

"That doesn't sound promising. You realize you could write your own ticket—and no, I'm not trying to lose you as an author, but I happen to like you a lot as a person, and I won't be the reason you can't find somebody to share your life with."

And it makes me wonder if he's in love. His whole way of thinking has flipped upside down.

"Thanks, Blake. I really appreciate all of it."

Chapter Thirteen

AS IT TURNS out, the interview scheduled for the morning following my conversation with Blake is one he personally set up with a friend of his, the owner of some media empire who's probably as wealthy as he is.

In other words, it's a cakewalk, completely in my favor. Sometimes, it's nice to know the guy at the top.

Wait, who am I kidding? It's always nice to know the guy at the top.

Even without being aware of the setup in advance, I felt a lot more comfortable this time around, thanks to Blake's assurances. Sure enough, the rest of the world is starting to figure out what a jerk Dustin Grant is. What a liar he is.

If he had only kept his mouth shut and minded his own business, he wouldn't be facing a crushing lawsuit. Matt told me all about that this morning after checking the news, like he always does way before I even consider lifting an eyelid.

Knowing Dustin is getting what he deserves makes sitting in front of yet another camera, after having my hair and makeup fussed with, a lot easier to deal with. If anything, I have to bite back a laugh when Dustin's name comes up.

Yes, I actually can be a little bitchy when I want to be.

Funny how I even have more energy and focus to devote to work now too.

ONCE THE INTERVIEW'S over in the morning, I spend time with my butt in my chair and finish my Santa story. Maggie will be thrilled.

If I never hear the words, *You know we're in a hurry to push this release*, again, I will be thankful.

And I'm starting to wonder if such a thing is possible.

I sit down for dinner with Matt. He is awesome and cooked for us to celebrate my turning in my book. *How sweet is that?*

"What do you think about me looking for a new publisher?" I ask him.

He pauses with his fork midair. Good thing the sauce on his pasta is so thick or else it would drip.

I sincerely wish I had known a long time ago that he was a good cook. All that money I've spent on takeout …

"You mean, what do I think about you doing exactly what I told you to do ages ago?"

He gets an eye roll for that one.

"Pat yourself on the back, why don't you?"

"I think I will." He finally puts the pasta in his

mouth, which at least gives me a few seconds where his mouth is full.

"I wouldn't have considered it if it hadn't been for Blake."

His eyes darken. "Blake, huh? So, when I suggested it, you ignored me. Or did you get mad at me? I barely remember."

Something tells me he remembers. The man has the memory of an elephant when he feels like it.

"I got mad at you because you were telling me what to do and I didn't like your tone."

"But you liked Blake's tone, huh?"

"I didn't bring this up to start an argument. I actually want your opinion. If you still think I should give it a shot."

"Of course I think you should give it a shot. I think it's the only fair thing to do for yourself." He puts down the fork and leans across his dining room table. He actually has a dining room table, like a grown-up. "But I was thinking about this date-and-write idea. It certainly has taken your sales in an upward trajectory."

"That's true."

"And now that your name is even better known, thanks to this publicity, you have the upper hand in the negotiations. As you should."

"You believe that?" I ask.

"Wholeheartedly. You're worth a lot more than what you give yourself credit for."

"Now, let's back up a second. I give myself plenty of credit."

"It doesn't show."

"Well, you know, I don't, like, come out and brag on myself. But I know I'm a good writer."

"I guess all those times I've heard you cursing yourself out and wondering if you're supposed to be a writer or if you should set your laptop on fire—"

"Okay, I get it."

There's a twinkle in his eye when he picks up his fork. "You're the one in charge right now. This is exactly the right time for you to look around, see if anybody else would be interested in picking up your contract. Talk to Lois. Isn't that what she does for a living?"

"I don't know. I'll have to ask her."

He chokes a little but recovers quickly enough. "How much would you bet she's already fielded at least one offer from another publisher?"

That's enough to stop me in my tracks. "You think so? No. No, that's not true. She would tell me if it was true."

"Have you asked her?"

"No."

"You should. I bet you'll see how right I am. Yet again."

"Do you not know better by now than to mock me when I'm holding a knife?"

He scoffs, rolling his eyes. "Please. You're all talk. If you intended to make good on your threats, you would've stabbed me a hundred times by now."

"How do you know I haven't used up all my self-control, and now, there's no telling the bloody rampage I'll go on?" Light glints off the knife as I wave it around. "I have a hundred stabs saved up, babe. You've been warned."

His wicked grin tells me I've said something he can turn dirty. The man has a one-track mind. "I have something I could stab you with a hundred times."

"You make it sound so romantic." Though I can't lie. My heart flutters a little. Maybe one day, the fact that I have sex with him won't seem like such a big deal, but this is not that day.

The wickedness fades a little before he says, "I'll make a bet with you."

"Okay. I think."

"Talk to Lois. Ask her if anybody's reached out with an offer to speak with you or questions about whether you're available to write for them instead."

"Fine. That sounds reasonable." I bet he's wrong. I bet nobody has. With that in mind, I'm fairly confident when I ask, "What's at stake?"

He gives me a grin. "Hmm. Good question. If I'm right, you have to … hmm …" His eyebrows move up and down.

"Fine, fine. I get the idea. And if I'm right—"

"Which you won't be."

"You have to cook six more dinners like this for me."

"Wow. You want six dinners, and all I want is—"

"Hey," I offer with a shrug, spearing a few pieces of penne. "Not my fault you need to think bigger."

"Actually," he says with a smirk, "I have been."

I give him a glare. "Why do you look so sneaky?"

"Not sneaky. Just decisive. And I didn't want to tell you about it until I was sure."

"Sure of what?"

He stands up, and pulls me up. He leans in and kisses me. "I'm going to have to show you."

I think he's talking about sex, so I'm not surprised when he takes me into his bedroom. But then I notice the big X on the wall.

"Do I want to know what that's for?" I say, trying to be sexy when I have no idea what is going on.

"I think so. Remember when you mentioned living together, but you didn't quite get the answer that I think you were looking for at the time?"

"Yeah?"

"Well, I've been thinking about it. And acting upon it. I think us moving in together is a great idea, but I think because we both work from home that we need our separate spaces. So, I got approval from the co-op board, and this wall is coming down tomorrow."

"Coming down? Like, to combine our apartments?"

"Exactly!" he says excitedly. Then, he grabs a

rolled-up set of papers and unfurls them across his bed. "I had plans drawn up. As long as you approve, I've hired a contractor friend who will make us living together a reality. And he is going to work overtime with a large crew to get almost all of it done before Christmas. Well, most of it. Everything but the kitchen."

"We're getting a new kitchen?" I say, suddenly dreaming of one like Kylie's.

"Yes, but not until later. Phase one, option one would include knocking down the wall joining our bedrooms and making one huge bedroom, expanding our his-and-hers closets and updating what would be his-and-hers bathrooms." He switches to a different sheet. "This is option two—and honestly my vote. Big bedroom. One massive, luxurious shared bathroom. Look at this. A fireplace in front of the tub. Can you imagine how romantic that would be?"

"I can. I like it. How did you come up with this all so fast?"

"My friend is good at what he does. I gave him some ideas, and he brought this back the next day."

"What about finishes, colors, all that?"

"His wife, Barbara, is a designer. All you have to do is call her, maybe show her your dream bath, and she'll work with you to make it happen."

"I like the shared-bath idea," I tell him.

"It's my favorite as well. We'd keep our separate offices as is, although if you wanted to paint or redecorate, now's the time."

"What else?" I ask, looking down and trying not to practically cry at the thought of all this. "It's like a dream come true."

"He thinks we should redo my kitchen and dining room, and then in that area in your place, I was thinking it would be cool to change it to kind of a hangout area. Maybe a pool table, big screen, bar. Like your grandmother's billiards room. Classy, functional."

"That sounds amazing. It would be so fun to have people over. Family. Friends."

"And the best part," he says, flipping a page and showing me a mock-up.

"It's like something out of my dreams!" I screech. "My very own library?"

"Yes, it wouldn't be your office. It's more a place to relax. Read. Sit in with a cup of coffee and look out the window."

"You're saying they can have all that done before Christmas?"

"He says yes. He does those home shows where they bring a big crew in and redo it in a short time. He says it will be a piece of cake."

I throw my arms around his neck. "You're amazing, Matt. The answer is yes. I want to combine our apartments. I want to live with you." I don't add *and live happily ever after*, but I think it.

"I want that too," he says with a grin as he kisses me. But then he stops and says, "But I was just thinking, since you're done with your book, are you planning to spin again?"

I scrunch up my face. "I thought we didn't want that?"

"We don't want you dating, but I was thinking since the Santa book practically *wrote itself* that, well"—he goes over to a drawer and pulls out a piece of paper—"what do you say we do another trope?"

"Um …"

He studies the paper. "I was doing a little research and wrote down a bunch. Let's see what's on here—oh, Flight Attendant." He sidles up to me and says, "Well, Kitty, I most certainly can give you a good layover."

I can't help but laugh. "You're funny."

"What else do we have? Oh, here's an easy one: Single Dog Dad. Too bad you haven't done that one yet. Hello, doggy style!"

"Matt!" I let out a girlie screech as he grabs my ass.

"Fine. We meet at the park."

"What are you saying?"

"I'm saying, you don't have to stop writing tropes just because we're together. Miss Valentine, my life is about research. Researching companies to see if they will be investment worthy. There's no reason you can't choose a trope, let me know, and I can do a little research. Hell, I'll even figure out a meet-cute for us. That's what they call it, right?"

I nod my head.

"You know how people go out separately and pretend to be strangers who meet at a bar to spice up their sex life? Not that ours will need spicing up—ever."

"Ever?" I wonder aloud.

"Never. And I was just thinking that I have no problem being, what shall we call me? Your research assistant. No, your trope whore."

"You'd do that for me?"

"I'd do that for *us*," he says before leading me to bed.

AFTER AN EXTREMELY good layover, I'm lying in bed, next to a sleeping Matt, staring at the X on the wall and having a mini freak-out.

"What if we don't work out?" I say out loud. "We put the wall back up?"

He rolls over and pulls me close to him. "Fine, but if we do, I get the side with the kitchen."

"Which means I'd be at your place all the time, so I could eat."

"And we'd be right back where we are now," he says. "I love you, Kitty."

"I love you too, Matt."

Chapter Fourteen

"SO, MATT, HAVE you given any thought to making an honest woman out of my granddaughter?"

"Well, so long, happy family dinner."

We literally just took off our coats, and already, I'm going back to the rack to pull them down. It has to be a record. The woman couldn't even wait until we had pre-dinner drinks or took a seat, for Pete's sake.

"Come on now." Peter manages to hold me back before I can bolt out the door. He leans in and whispers in my ear, "She told me she was going to do that as soon as you came in. Don't pay her any mind. She wants to tease Matt to see how well he handles himself."

I should've known she would do something like that. I mean, I know the woman well enough by now.

Meanwhile, Matt's handling things like a champ. He basically ignored my reaction in favor of addressing my grandmother's little remark. "Do you think your granddaughter is dishonest? Have I done something to make her that way?"

Maybe it's the way he said it or the bottle of her favorite wine he's carrying in one hand. Maybe it's his charm. Goodness knows, I've fallen victim to it. The man is dangerous when he wants to be.

Either way, she laughs. "If you've been doing your job properly, you have."

"Oh my God." I cover my eyes with my hand while Peter pats me on the back, the two of us still standing just outside the dining room.

"She likes him. Very much. So do I, for what it's worth. He seems like a good man."

"He is." I look at him with a smile. "I guess it takes one to know one, huh?"

"I'm another story." He winks and then tips his head toward the room, where my grandmother is practically giggling over something Matt told her. I mean, the woman is giggling like a teenager.

"What are you two talking about?" I wind my arm around Matt's and stare at the woman who clearly considers it her life's mission to humiliate me.

"Oh, nothing very important." But another giggle bubbles up from her just the same.

When she turns away to hand the bottle of wine to Frank, her newish butler, Matt murmurs, "I told her I don't care much for honest women, but if it makes her happy, I'll think about it. She said she's never cared much for them either, so it's a good thing she isn't one."

"She's in a real mood tonight."

"I think she's happy; that's all. And glad to have you here."

The woman finally gets around to kissing my cheek, which she didn't have a chance to do before deliberately embarrassing me. "You look wonderful, dear."

I swear on all that's holy and otherwise, if she makes a remark about it being because I'm getting laid on the regular, I will cancel the entire holiday. But she doesn't. She leaves the compliment where it is.

"Thank you. So do you." I touch a finger to the sleeve of her deep purple cashmere sweater, which, for some people, would be super dressy, but for her, it's downright casual. "Is this a new holiday look for you? I agree with it."

"I thought I would dress more comfortably tonight. Wouldn't want to intimidate your young man."

"That was obvious from the way you flat-out told him he'd better marry me. No pressure there at all."

"Oh, that." She waves a hand. "That's a grandmother's privilege."

"Embarrassing her granddaughter?"

She nods, solemn. "You'll understand one day—if the two of you get down to business, that is."

"Can we not talk about me getting down to business, please? And I swear, if you say anything to him about any such thing"—I hold a finger up in her face and do my best to look menacing—"I will leave. And I'll take the wine and maybe a pie with me."

She nods slowly, and anybody who knows her could tell she's pretending to be serious and intimidated. "Of course, dear. Whatever you say."

I mean, what did I expect?

"I assume you finished your book?" Grandmother directs me to my seat at the table, which has the leaf removed so we can all sit closer to each other.

The table is set impeccably, as always, but there's something different about it. Something homier, warmer. Less silver and crystal, more flowers and gourds.

Though we'll still be eating off the good china. The woman hasn't lowered her standards that much.

"Yes. I wrote this one quite quickly."

"Well, I'm sure some sexy inspiration helped in that matter," Grandmother says.

My eyes go wide.

Matt clears his throat as he takes his seat across from me. "I thought we weren't going to talk about work tonight?"

"She might have made that promise to you, young man, but I have made no such vow." Grandmother takes her seat before ringing the small silver bell positioned in front of her plate, and when Frank pokes his head into the room, she asks for the soup to be served.

"Honestly, there isn't much to talk about anyway. I finished the book, and now"—I shrug, looking around the table—"we'll see how this surprise-release thing does."

"I don't know much about the publishing business, I admit, but it seems to me you won't have much trouble with that after the publicity you've received." Peter offers a faint smile. "I realize it hasn't done you any favors in your personal life, but it might mean a great deal more success in other areas."

Matt's right though. I don't want to talk about work tonight. I'm tired of talking about myself as a whole. Which is why I ask, "Are you two planning on doing any more traveling? Since you had so much fun on your honeymoon."

"We've been discussing that now that you mention it. Peter has a list of places he'd like to visit." Grandmother's eyes twinkle when she grins across the table.

"Oh? Like where?"

He shrugs with a shy little chuckle. "I've been an avid fan of travel shows for years now. I used to love the chef who visited various countries and sampled their food and spoke about culture and political history. I watched that show religiously."

"Which means he created a list of places he liked best."

Peter lowers his brow. "I did no such thing."

"But you have ideas. There's nothing wrong with that. We have all the time in the world to explore. I want you to have what you want, darling."

Matt and I exchange a look. I can tell he finds this just as cute as I do.

Peter makes a gruff sort of throat-clearing sound. "As you can see, we've had this discussion already."

"I think it's a great idea. You should explore the world together. Have fun, get in a little trouble, eat … I don't know … brains or something."

Frank stumbles a little as he comes around, collecting the soup bowls. I shoot him an apologetic look. It seems I have a habit of shocking servers and servants.

"Sorry," I whisper when he reaches me.

Grandmother chuckles wryly. "I can't say that's a notion I've ever entertained. Though I would be willing to visit a place where they serve them. Perhaps."

The idea of my Chanel-clad, pearl-wearing grandmother sitting in a hole-in-the-wall restaurant in some remote town doesn't want to form itself into an actual mental image. Certain things just don't compute.

The fact that she's willing to entertain the idea tells me how she's grown. How her relationship with Peter has changed her, softened her, left her open to greater possibilities than dining at The

Plaza with her so-called friends and attending one charity function after another.

Who am I kidding—attending? She planned them. Ruled over her social circle.

Now, she wants something new. Something better. I, for one, am fully behind her. If it means talking Peter into allowing her to take him around the world, so be it.

The food is delicious, as usual.

"Frank, this looks incredible," I say.

"Thank you. Though I can't take full credit." He slides a look toward Peter before going back to the kitchen to grab more food.

I turn to him with my brows raised. "And what does that mean?"

"I might have shared a few tips." He lifts his shoulders. "Well? Do you know how many of these dinners I've prepared? He doesn't even do the cooking himself. Has other people come in to help him." The sourness in his voice tells me all I need to know about his opinions on this.

Matt bites back a grin. "Old habits are hard to break."

Grandmother arches an eyebrow. "What of your old habits, Matt? Is there anything I should know about?"

"Cecile." Peter shakes his head while I fight the urge to slide down in my chair.

"Well? I have a right to know who my grand-daughter is seriously involved with. It was one thing to know she was casually dating those young men, but this is something different."

Matt's much better at this than I am. Rather than shrinking or cringing or rolling his eyes, he answers straight out, "I don't have a lot of bad habits. I don't smoke. I rarely drink. No drugs. I'm fairly disciplined."

"I can tell that much." She winks at him and basically makes me want to die.

A glance at Peter tells me he knows her well enough by now to take this in stride.

Matt clears his throat—and is that a flush on his cheeks? I'll never let him live it down—yes, I know that makes me a lot more like my grandmother than I want to admit. So, sue me.

"He's the real deal," I assure her. "He's a good one. He makes me look downright lazy and slovenly."

"You're not so bad," Matt offers.

"Oh, how generous of you."

"I have a good feeling about this. Watching you two together." Peter stands up, knife in hand, ready to carve the turkey. "I have a feeling this is the first of many family dinners we'll be spending together."

Matt smiles at me from across the table, and yes, now that I think about it, I can imagine seeing him sitting with me at many family dinners to come. Maybe the rest of them, all my life.

"They put a hole in our wall today," I blurt out.

"Why ever for?" Grandmother says.

"We're combining our apartments. We're going to live together."

"Really?" Grandmother says. "That's a big commitment."

"Yes, it is," Matt says, squeezing my hand. "One we both take very seriously."

"We're very happy for the two of you," Peter says sweetly.

Dinner goes on and on. In a good way. In the kind of way that, even when it's getting late, you're just not quite ready to leave because you don't want the night to be over. We drink wine, and then Matt teaches us how to play pinochle. Then, he manages to beat Grandmother.

She jokes he is never to be invited again. At least, I think she is joking.

ON THE WAY home, sitting together in the car, Matt turns to me. "It's beautiful, seeing them so happy and in love, isn't it?"

I've never heard him talk that way before. "Yeah, it is. I feel very full right now."

"You had two helpings of dessert."

"I don't mean, in my stomach, silly. I mean, here." I put a hand over my heart. "I feel full here."

"That's nice. That's how it should be." He drapes an arm over my shoulders and pulls me close while our driver takes us home. "I'm glad it didn't take us thirty-six years to decide to get together."

"That's the truth. I don't know if I could stand you for thirty-six years and still want to be in a relationship with you when all was said and done."

"Does that mean you don't see us lasting for very long?" he teases.

"No!"

"Because, you know, I could start looking at other options. I mean, if anything, tonight, your grandmother let me know what a catch I am. She asked how much I make a year when you went to the bathroom between dinner and dessert."

"She did not."

"She did. And she seemed pleased with the answer. Between that and informing me how it looks like I'm disciplined—I think we both know that means she likes my bod—"

"I'm sure she does. It is pretty amazing," I coo. "Everything with you is pretty amazing. And I think you need to remind me of that when we get home."

"Home," he says. "With the wall gone, technically, we can say that now, can't we?"

"That's reason enough to celebrate," I tell him.

Chapter Fifteen

HAYLEY'S MOUTH HANGS open, her eggs Benedict forgotten in front of her. "Matt punched a hole through your wall?"

"He didn't personally, but he had a friend draw up these amazing plans. Our apartment is going to be so cool. We'll have to tackle the kitchen after the holidays, but—"

"But nothing. This is huge. You're moving in together. That's a serious commitment."

"The funny thing is, we really didn't talk about it. I floated the idea, and when he said he'd think about it, I assumed that was his polite way of telling me no. When he showed me the plans, I thought I might faint."

"Excuse me." A middle-aged woman comes over to our table with a shy smile. "I just wanted to tell you, I think it was rotten the way that has-been tried to drag your reputation through the muck. I hope they hang him by the balls for it."

Hayley laughs behind her hand while I do everything I can to keep a straight face.

"I appreciate that."

"Well, that's it, I guess."

One of her friends is motioning to her, probably begging her to go back to her table before everybody's embarrassed.

"Happy holidays," she offers before hurrying back to her friends and their shopping bags.

"Nothing like sharing holiday cheer." Hayley giggles. "At least you know there are people who saw through his bullshit."

"I'm sure plenty of people did—though I wish I could go back to having brunch with you without having to wonder whether a stranger is going to come over out of nowhere."

"That'll die down. Wait and see." She goes back to her eggs, eyeing me as she cuts into them. "So, tell me more. Like, are you painting everything?"

I roll my eyes at her. "I am working with a designer. I tell her what I want, send her some pics for inspiration, and she's going to make it happen."

"Oh, that's the best way to do it. And I'm saying that as a friend because I clearly remember going to the paint store with you." She smiles mockingly and pretends to speak in my voice. "*I'd like Tiffany blue, but not quite Tiffany blue. A little more green—no, a little less green. Maybe a little gray in there.*"

"Be nice."

"I'm just saying, I wouldn't wish that on Matt," she teases. At least, I think she's teasing.

"We're working with a designer. I pinned my dream rooms and inspirational ideas to a board and sent it to her, and she sent me back a mood board that I approved quickly because it was perfection. When I get back home, I'll have a few samples to look at and paint swatches to approve, but she's picked out everything, including an incredible four-poster bed. I've always thought those are so romantic. But enough about me. How are you? How are you feeling? Any morning sickness?"

"So far, so good. As long as I eat as soon as I get up, I'm okay. That part of it has gone smoothly. And I had my first visit with an obstetrician, who confirmed the pregnancy and gave us a due date."

"A due date," I say with a happy sigh.

"Yes, and I realized that all the other stuff doesn't matter. We'll figure it out. We're both going to put in for transfers to each other's offices as well as look for new opportunities. Nicholas surprisingly really liked New York City, but he thinks we should be in the suburbs to raise our family. I'm embarrassed to say, I didn't know this, but his grandparents had a house on the Cape, and he spent many summers there. He thinks we should consider Massachusetts or Connecticut. We really can't both work eighty-hour weeks with a baby. Well, we could, but we don't want to."

"That's amazing, Hayley."

"It's shit," she says. "Years of school, law school, studying to get to where I am, and now, I'm considering throwing it all away."

"You're not throwing it all away. You're designing your life. With Nicholas. Together. You just have to figure out a different work-life balance. It will happen. But I admit, I like the idea of you being not quite so far away."

"That's true. And I do too. It's the not knowing that's hard."

"But it also gives you time to think. Had you not had some time to think, had you not gotten pregnant, you would have moved out to LA and fallen into the same rut of work, work, work. You would have been happy, being with Nicholas, but—"

"I get what you're saying. And you're right."

"Wow! You want to say that again, so I can record it for posterity?"

"August 4th," she says.

"What's that got to do with anything?"

"It's the date you're going to become a godmother."

"A godmother? Like a fairy one?"

"If need be. But I want you to be my child's godmother. So, I'm asking you now."

Tears fill my eyes, and I reach across the table and grab her hand. "I'd be honored."

"Good," she says. "Now, you'd better get going, so you aren't late for your meeting with Lois. Be bold."

"I will," I say.

"As a matter of fact, yes, I've received a few unsolicited offers," Lois says to me when I get to her office.

I plop down on the couch, and a sound I don't quite recognize comes out of me. Something between a grunt and a gasp. "You're kidding."

"I thought I would tell you about it after the holidays. So you could have time to work on your latest book without having this on your mind."

That makes me laugh, though there isn't any humor in it. "I do wish you'd let me know people were interested. Especially since I turned the book in already."

She pauses a beat. "Are you considering making a change?"

The whole thing just makes me cringe. I feel bad about even considering it. *If it wasn't for them, where would I be?* I feel like I owe my career to them. But I'm going to be a godmother, and I have to be bold. I'm the one who creates the content they are selling. I'm the talent.

"I want you to tell me of any offer that comes my way."

"I really wish you had told me this was on your mind. You and Maggie seem to have a good relationship. I figured you'd tell me it was a hard no."

Ugh, she's so exhausting—and right, which makes her even more exhausting to me at the moment.

"Fair enough, but with all the publicity, I think it's worth considering. If ever there was a time to make a move, it's now. My sales are great." Another beat. "Wait. Are you keeping something from me now?"

"No, I'm not hiding anything. But there is another issue I wanted to bring up after the holidays."

"I would rather discuss it now."

"Well, your current publisher knows a good thing when they see it. Your sales are good in the States as well as many foreign markets. You're not just a *New York Times* best seller, Kitty. You're hitting lists worldwide. An *international* best seller. With that in mind, they're interested in offering you a contract for another ten books."

Ten books. That's a lot. And a big commitment. I think about Hayley and how she wants to slow down and have a life. I want to do the same. Have an amazing life with Matt. But I'm getting ahead of myself. I told Maggie what books I wanted to write. She gave me her word that I could go back to writing sweet. I need to find out the terms of the deal.

Which is why I ask, "And what kind of books am I to write?"

"I thought that was a given. More of the tropes, of course."

I know Matt said he'd help me research, but I don't want that pressure.

"It's not where my heart is. It's not what I want to write. And I can't keep up this kind of writing schedule. And I won't."

"Sweetheart, right now, you could write about a restaurant, and you'd end up with a best seller. But what's the real reason? You fall for one of the guys you wrote about?"

"No, but I am in a relationship right now, and dating other guys would kind of ruin it. So, why do I feel like I don't have any say in this?"

"You do—it's called negotiation. We'll go back to the publisher and state our demands. I'm with you, doll. I think you've given them their pound of flesh and then some. It's time for you to start calling the shots."

"I think I needed to hear that from you. Thank you, Lois."

"That's what I'm here for. You know you've been my easiest, least fussy client from the start. You deserve to work on your own terms now after everything you've been through."

"I have to agree."

"You have a face-to-face with Maggie soon. After, if you don't want to continue the relationship, I'll put out feelers."

"I think you should actually start putting them out now," I say boldly.

AND NOW, IT looks like I owe Matt something. Sure, I know what he has in mind, but there's something I've had on my mind for a long time. Something I owe him.

After my meeting with Lois is over, I go to a

store with a good selection of what I'm looking for.

When they ask if I want it delivered, I tell them, "No, thank you. I'll carry it."

They look at me like I'm crazy, and I probably am.

But it feels like the right thing to do.

I throw the thing over my shoulder and trudge home. Manage to get it up the stairs. Then knock on his door. I know it's unlocked, but I want the visual.

Matt opens the door, takes one look at me, and bursts out laughing. "Finally. You're finally replacing my rug."

But it's me who gets a shock. Matt is basically naked. Wearing only a tool belt around his waist and an orange hard hat on his head.

"Told you I would."

"Does this mean, I won the bet?"

"Yep."

"So, I dressed up for nothing?"

"More like didn't get dressed," I tease, stepping into the disaster that is currently our place.

"I've got power tools," he says. "I can drill." He pulls a hammer up out of the tool belt and tosses it in the air before catching it. "Oh, and yes, I have a hammer. Need anything hammered, ma'am?"

He tips the hard hat, and I notice it's not the only hard thing on his body.

I drop the rug onto the floor. It can wait.

"Actually, I do," I say, sauntering over to him as I shed my own clothing. "It will have to be quick though, before my boyfriend comes home, you strong, studly—" I start laughing. "Get it? *Studly?* Like the wall studs."

"Oh, I get it," Matt says, closing the space between us. "And now, you're going to get it too."

Chapter Sixteen

THE SECOND I see my grandmother's number on my phone, my chest goes tight. That's always the way it goes. I can't *not* worry about her when she calls at random times.

She's not the one doing the calling though. If anything, hearing Peter when I pick up only makes my chest clench tighter than before. I can barely breathe.

"What's wrong?"

"Nothing's wrong, nothing at all. I was only wondering ... are you free for lunch today?"

Even if I had plans, which I don't since the house is a disaster and I won't start writing another book until after the new year, I would still say, "Sure. Just tell me the time and the place."

But he's never had lunch with just me before, and I get the feeling that there's something he's not telling me.

"I thought perhaps I might bring something over for us to share. I ... know you've had trouble recently, being noticed in public."

"Of course, you're welcome to come over, but

just know with the remodeling going on, it's loud and chaotic here."

"I'm sure it will be fine," he says.

We end the call, and I dramatically throw myself across the couch, where Matt is watching some game.

"I'm sure everything is fine," Matt says. "Maybe it's about a Christmas surprise he wants to plan for your grandmother. Or it could be something he knows she's planning for you that he thinks you won't like."

"Or she could be keeping something from me. Like her heart's gotten worse."

"Kitty."

I do love hearing him say my name. Seriously, I never get tired of the way it rolls off his lips. How, sometimes, the way he says it is soothing. Sometimes totally sexy. Sometimes funny. Although, usually, when he's being a smart-ass, he calls me Valentine.

He pauses the game and pulls me into his arms, causing me to sigh. "I know you love her, and that's why you worry. She means a lot to you. I happen to be very fond of her myself."

"I know you are." I close my eyes and breathe deep, inhaling his scent. It calms me. So does Phoebe's gentle nudging against my leg.

"Do you have something to say about it?" I ask her, reaching down to pet her silky fur. She's like living, breathing therapy.

I can handle this. Whatever Peter wants to talk about, I can handle it. And for all I know, Matt might be right.

"I'm going to take Phoebe for a walk, so you two can have your privacy." He gives me a sweet kiss as Phoebe prances toward the door.

The remodel has been hard on all of us but especially her. She is used to long naps during the day, and there's just too much excitement going on.

BY THE TIME Peter arrives, I have the place tidied up as best as it can be and have set the table with a tablecloth and everything. I want him to feel comfortable amid the chaos that is this renovation. At least we aren't doing anything to Matt's kitchen or dining room just yet, so it's sort of our safe space. Granted, it's dusty, and I had to scrub it all down. And luckily for us, the timing works. Most of the workers have gone for lunch.

"Oh, this is beautiful," he says once he's in the dining room. He admires the tree, the wreaths, the draped garland Matt helped me hang around the windows. The room is fully decked out since it's the only room we decorated. "Your grandmother would love to see this."

"I'll invite her over." I motion to the table. "So, what did you bring for lunch?"

When he starts pulling dishes out of a bag, the sight of homemade egg salad sandwiches makes me clap my hands. The man knows me, and he knows that his egg salad is my favorite thing to eat during my weekly teas with Grandmother.

"I brought extra in a container for you to put in the fridge."

"You're the best!"

He also brought a fruit salad and cookies for dessert, which he sets down on the table with all the careful consideration of a retired butler while I pour white wine for both of us.

Egg salad and white wine. We are truly living large. Though to be fair, he finds a way to elevate it. Fresh dill, shallots chopped so fine that they're practically invisible. Same with the celery. A little mayo, a little Dijon, lots of salt and pepper. The aroma alone makes my mouth water.

"Well"—I sit across from him and raise my glass—"what should we toast to?"

"The holidays," he says. "It's a wondrous time of the year. Especially here in New York City."

But when his smile fades, I can't hold back any longer.

"All right, spill. What's the matter?"

His eyes widen. I remember when he was younger and his gray hair was still black. He's one of the only constants in my life. Really, he's sort of acted as my grandfather since I never got to meet mine.

He chuckles with a wry expression. "You are so much like her. I often wonder if she was like you at your age."

"You've seen pictures of her, right?"

"Yes, and the resemblance is striking. The same hair, the same eyes."

"And she's still sharp as a tack."

His smile falters, and that's when I know I'm in for something I absolutely don't want to hear. But if he's brave enough to reach out to me and put this little lunch together, I'm brave enough to listen with my whole heart.

Besides, if there's something wrong with her, he's probably aching for somebody to talk to.

"You remember the discussion we had the other night, I'm sure."

I try to crack a smile along with a joke. "The one about how much Matt makes?"

He laughs softly at that. "Told you about that, did he? She means well."

"Oh, I know she does."

"I wasn't referring to that though. I was referring to the travel talk."

"Okay," I say, only now, I'm really worried. Because he looks worried.

"I don't want to upset you."

"Oh no." I set the sandwich down.

"No, no, please. Forgive me. I'm so clumsy when it comes to these things. I suppose I'm used to your grandmother doing the talking for me. After so many years, you learn what the other is thinking without having to be told. She finishes my sentences before I've even fully formed them in my mind. It might be for the best for her to stay home from now on. At least, to stay in the city and get her rest."

"Her heart."

He sighs and hesitates but nods. "There were a few times during our trip when her color seemed off and she got overly tired."

"I wondered if the trip would be too much for her."

"Well, you know her. There's no convincing her to take it easy. I did, however, convince her to visit her doctor when we got home. He suggested that she dial back her physical activity for a while."

"How did she take that?"

"Do you really need to ask?"

"I guess not."

Knowing her, she probably signed up for a 5K immediately on getting home, just to prove a point. Maybe we're more alike than I've previously admitted now that I think about it.

"I didn't want you to think I was ungrateful toward her, the way she offered to help my travel dreams become a reality. I'm not that stubborn. I'm only worried about her."

This I can handle. So long as she hasn't gotten any worse.

I go back to the sandwich, thinking as I chew. "You know she'd hate it if she knew you were digging in your heels because of her health."

"She knows."

"She does? And she's still being impossible?

Right. Of course she is. Pretend I didn't ask that."

"She refuses to accept the doctor's orders. And mind you, he didn't make it sound like a life-or-death situation. He suggested she take it easy and not tax herself for no reason."

More chewing. More thinking.

"I have to talk through something going on in my head. I hope you don't mind," I finally say.

"Not at all." If anything, he looks glad to be finished speaking for a while. Now, he can get into actually eating his lunch.

"Okay, so my immediate impulse is to side with you a hundred percent—please, let me work it through before you say anything." I hate to even think it, but the poor man is used to having to hold his tongue while a woman speaks her mind. "Like I said, I want to side with you. As far as I'm concerned, she should be locked in her room and monitored around the clock to make sure she's not going against her doctor's orders. If I had my way, she'd move into a single-floor home, so she wouldn't have to use the stairs at all. Someplace smaller while we're at it. Less walking around. I know she'd hate it, but it would be for her own good." I pick at what's left of half my sandwich and sigh. "But if someone told me what to do, I would not be happy about it."

"You're right, of course."

"And I can see the dilemma since we both want what's best. But what is best really? We all have a limited amount of time on this earth. And I shouldn't tell her what to do. We can't tell her what to do. We have to make her want to do what's good for her. You're a brave man, Peter," I say with a laugh because Grandmother can be quite the handful.

"I'm a very lucky man. Your grandmother is a remarkable woman who I have the honor of loving. I suppose Matt and I have that much in common. We both love remarkable women."

"What if you suggested shorter trips? Like a ten-day stay in Tokyo rather than over three weeks of touring various European sites? All the traveling from one place to another probably took its toll."

"I imagine it did. She insisted though."

"Big surprise. I think it's a fair compromise—a shorter trip, one location, and she can rest a little when she needs to. And she gets to experience it all with you. If that goes well, you can take another trip and another one, and pretty soon, you'll have had adventures all over the world."

"Safe ones."

"Safe ones, of course."

"You're right." He looks and sounds so relieved now. "I'm sure she'll agree to that. And if she doesn't want to behave herself, we can sit in the hotel every day until it's time to go."

She'll never go for that, but I don't have the heart to say it.

WE HAVE A nice time, chatting about the upcoming holidays, and Peter is sounding much better than when he first arrived.

"I'm so glad you came over," I tell him. "And that you brought the egg salad. Matt and I will be living on it until it's gone."

I walk with him toward the front door, but before he leaves, I grab him in an impulsive hug. "I love you. I don't know if I've ever said that to you, but I thought you should know. Not just because of who you are to her, but because of who you are, period."

When I let him go, his eyes are a little brighter, a little shinier than before. "And I love you. I've always thought of you as a granddaughter."

"I know," I say, feeling emotional.

Good thing Matt walks in when he does. "Good to see you, Peter," he says, setting down the bag he's carrying so he can shake Peter's hand.

They chat for a minute before Peter says, "Your grandmother will be getting back from having lunch and playing cards with her friends soon, and I will be honest, I didn't tell her about our lunch plans," and then bids us farewell.

When we're alone, Matt raises his brow, leaning against the doorframe with his arms folded. "So? How'd it go?"

"Okay. Grandmother overdid it a little on their trip, so Peter and I worked out a plan so that they could keep traveling in a way that would be *less stressful* to her heart. You would've been proud of me. I didn't freak. Who knows? Maybe Kitty Valentine has finally grown up."

"I hope not too much," he teases before giving me a kiss. "Because Phoebe and I brought you a surprise." He picks the bag he brought in and hands it to me.

"Oh, Matt!" I squeal. "Peppermint bark, home-made toffee, sugared pecans, and candy canes! I love all those!" I dig deeper and pull out a DVD. "And these are all the animated Christmas shows that were on television when I was a kid. Rudolph and Frosty were always my favorite!"

"I thought we could spend the rest of the day in front of the fire, snuggled up and watching them."

I turn around and look around at the plastic tarps covering most everything around us.

"That sounds perfect. Any chance you might put on the Santa suit again?" I ask.

"Hmm … that could probably be arranged."

Chapter Seventeen

"SO, YOU'RE MEETING with Maggie this afternoon, right?" Matt asks as I'm trying to get myself to look decent even though, currently, we only have running water in the kitchen.

"How many more days do we have left?" I ask. Last I heard there were three. Or six maybe. Depending on if all the supplies came in on time.

His contractor friend has been amazing. Old walls are gone. New walls are being built. Painting started very early this morning. I've never seen a project move so fast. Well, except on those house shows, which I am basically living right now. Although I'm pretty sure those people move out.

"Not too many. And they're installing the tub and tiling today. So, Matt and I were thinking," Jack says.

Jack is the general contractor, and I'm wondering what decision they made without me. I really can't complain though. I'm happy with how it's all turning out. And I can't wait for my library to be complete. We decided not to make it like Grandmother's with its dark wood and heavy furniture. The designer, Barbara, saw the color of my office and decided to play off it. The library cabinets are all going to be painted a gorgeous dark blue gray. And don't even get me started on the bold wallpaper she chose. Pretty much, the decision-making process has involved me jumping up and down and clapping with excitement. Matt has been more practical about things. He's all into the details. Like how much water pressure the showerhead will have, being able to control all the lights in the house with his phone, and the felt on the pool table.

"What were you thinking?" I ask.

"That you should move into a hotel for a few days while we get everything finished," Jack says.

I turn to Matt. "And you didn't think I would agree?"

Matt just shrugs, like he has no idea. But he does. He knows I'm not great with change. And he knows I'm going to see Maggie today, and depending how things go, that might involve a lot of change. And he probably knows it's better to just shrug than say what he really thinks and have me disagree.

Hmm. Maybe this whole relationship has a shot, long-term.

"Jack, I think it's a brilliant idea. Does that mean we can do one of those reveals, like they do on television?"

"It does," Jack says.

"Not washing my hair in the kitchen sink, room service, and a reveal? I'm in," I say happily. Really, I'm so happy right now, I can hardly stand myself.

But then I remember what I have to do today first.

"I told you she'd love it," Jack says, slapping Matt on the back with a smirk.

"I already made reservations and packed," Matt says, grinning back at him.

Jack goes back through the plastic barrier and chats with the crew. Matt pulls me into a hug.

"Why did you shrug if you'd already made reservations?" I ask. "Is it because you know I don't like surprises?"

"You have told me that before."

I nod, sliding my hands up his firm chest. "Well, you should know that I'm over that. You've cured me. I now love surprises. Especially when they are from you."

"I'm touched, Valentine." He slaps me on the ass and says, "Be strong today, and we'll celebrate at the hotel tonight."

I PRACTICALLY FLOAT to my appointment. *How could I not?* I feel like I'm a character in one of my books, living her perfect life. Granted, it's a bit of a mess right now, but how lucky are we that Matt had a friend who could pull this remodel off in such a condensed period of time? In a few days, we'll go back to a combined apartment that will be our home.

"So, are you really in love with your hot neighbor? Is he worth risking your career for?" are the first words out of Maggie's mouth.

I'm so stunned that all I can do is nod.

"The hot neighbor," she continues. "Let's go with that then. It can be your next trope."

"I'm keeping that one to myself," I say with a forced grin.

"Pity," she says. "Lois tells me that because of some man, you want to stop doing what's earning you money."

"No, because of a man, I made the decision to stop *dating* for research. I have also realized that I miss writing from my heart. The stories that speak to me, not the stories I'm *told* to write."

"What does that mean?"

"I want to write sweet again, Maggie. And although the steamier stuff is selling, since you made me get on social media, I'm getting a lot of messages from my readers who miss them. And if you don't agree—"

"What, did you fire Lois?"

"No, but I've been doing some research." Actually, Matt has done a ton of research. "And if you don't want my sweet stories or to pay me what they are worth, I'll find another publisher. Or self-publish. Go indie."

"What?" Maggie looks aghast. Like I just uttered a string of horrible curse words at her.

"Matt's a financial wizard. He's done projections, and honestly, between the cut you and Lois take, even if I didn't sell as many, I'd make twice as much, if not more. I'm not the wide-eyed college girl who was just thrilled to see my story on a bookstore shelf anymore."

"Oh, so it's all about the money now?" she chides.

I chuckle. "No, but it has always been about that for you. Money is the reason you sent me down this path. Money and the company's bottom line and your bonuses are what drive you. So, don't even *think* of questioning my love for writing. Because it's my love for writing—my passion for love stories—that *drives* me. Do I think my sweet loves stories will be a little spicier after this experiment? Yes. Have I grown through this? Yes. Have I learned to appreciate the art of writing sexy times? Yes. But the truth is, I like leaving something to the imagination. I like knowing just enough to tease, to take me down a path, and then letting my imagination do the rest. And there's a market for that."

"Does Lois know about this?"

"She knows how I feel, and she's had other inquiries that she's going to pursue. Although I appreciate that she helped negotiate my contracts, the fact that she gets a cut for the *lifetime* of the book, doing something a lawyer could have done for a flat fee, kind of makes me sick to my stomach. Times are changing, Maggie."

"Very clever," she says. "That's what I told you when we started the trope books, didn't I?"

"Yes."

"Hmm. So, in other words, Lois is out, shopping you and your next book to other publishers. She'll get a bidding war going. And it's a lose-lose for me."

I give her a shrug. I don't know where this confident Kathryn Valentine came from, but it feels good. If I were writing this in a book, I'd want to say it was from the love of a good man, but I know that's just part of it. The confidence has always been there. I mean, have you met my grandmother? She oozes the shit. And some of that must have gotten passed down to me. It just got buried a little after my parents died. But I can honestly say that, today, I'm proud to feel a little bit like her.

And I've also decided that if Matt and I ever get married, I am going to want the dream wedding, and I damn well know that she's going to help me plan it. And if she wants to pay for it because it brings her joy, I've decided I'm going to let her.

"I'll get back to you," Maggie finally says, ending our meeting.

I'M GETTING READY to catch a cab when my phone rings.

Blake Marlin. Interesting.

"Kitty Valentine," he says when I answer.

"Blake Marlin," I reply, still feeling cocky.

"I hear you're putting the screws in one of my companies."

And I swear, the second he says that, I think of Matt in nothing but a hard hat and a tool belt, and I nearly start giggling.

"Well, if you taught me anything, Blake, it was that *everything* is open for negotiation. Except with your mother."

This causes him to laugh out loud. "Damn straight." He's quiet for a moment then says wistfully, "I guess at least I can say, I was your first."

"We didn't sleep together, Blake, despite my attempts."

"I meant your first trope. But you are right. Business often gets in the way of my pleasure, but I'm working on that. Actually, because of you, I'm working less. Instead of twenty-four/seven, it's more like twenty-four/five. I'm trying to take the weekends off on a regular basis."

"Good for you."

"I shouldn't be telling you this because I'm eroding Maggie's bargaining ability, but you should know she's been given a blank check in regard to you. I don't want you to leave my company."

I'm stunned. "Uh, thank you."

"Trust me, Kitty, I know what's going on in the industry. I know you could probably make more as an independent, but I hope if the advances are high enough and the terms are to your satisfaction, you'll stay with us and let us handle the business side of things for you."

And I will admit, that's something that concerned me when Matt brought it up. I don't know if I want the hassle of owning a business or if I just want to write books.

"I hope that happens, too, Blake, and I'm happy you're taking some time off."

"Well, I met someone," he says.

"You did? Tell me all about her."

"She's a veterinarian. One of Mom's dogs got sick when I happened to be paying a visit, and when we met, it was …"

"Fate?" I venture.

"Something like that. I don't know; you're the writer. Anyway, I've been trying to get out there as much as possible to see her."

"I bet that makes your mom happy."

"Oh, she's in heaven."

I can believe that, thinking back on my visit to meet her and how much she clearly doted on her brilliant and successful son.

"I'm so glad, for all of you. Listen, if this veterinarian of yours can get you to relax and enjoy life a little, she has my approval."

"That means a lot."

I bite my lip before whispering, "To tell you the truth, I think I have found somebody. Somebody very special."

"Good for you, Kitty Valentine."

When we end the call, I think about the guys I've dated since this all started. I gave them all happy endings in my books, but I can't help but wonder how they are doing in real life.

Chapter Eighteen

W̲HEN I GET to the hotel, I'm told that Mr. Ryder and his *adorable* dog have already arrived.

Although when I open the door and see a beautiful suite laid out in front of me, I start to feel like *I've* arrived. I've never stayed in a room like this before.

Phoebe quickly greets me. She's got a chewy stick in her mouth, and she gives me a lick before taking it back in the living room, where she lies down in front of the expansive windows to chew on it.

Matt strides out of what I assume is the master bedroom, nothing but a towel wrapped around his waist. His hair is damp, and it's obvious he just got out of the shower.

"Oh, sure. I had to wash my hair in the kitchen sink this morning, and you're here in luxury."

"I splurged on a suite," he says. "You like it?"

I wrap my arms around his neck. "I haven't seen it all, so I'm not sure I can answer that question yet."

He sweeps me off my feet, carries me into the

bedroom, tosses me on the bed, and takes off the towel.

WE'RE LYING IN the comfortable bed—like, seriously, you just sink down into it and never want to leave—in the afterglow of amazing sex, when Matt says, "You like the suite now?"

"I still haven't seen the bathroom."

"It's beautiful, but I think ours will be better," he says, his face turning serious. "They don't have a fireplace."

"This was a good idea," I reply, my eyes taking in the ornate ceiling and chandelier above me.

"Agree. It's a pretty place. This bed is amazing, and one of the reasons I chose this hotel is because Jack's wife said they use the same beds that we are supposed to have in our room. She wanted us to make sure we liked it. Do we like it?"

I nuzzle up to his chest and run my fingers across it. "It's like sleeping on a cloud."

"We haven't done any sleeping yet," he teases.

"Still, can't you tell?"

"Yes, I can, and I agree. It's the most comfortable bed I've ever been in."

"Way better than being surrounded by plastic tarps and sleeping on a mattress on the dining room floor," I say. "And Phoebe is thrilled to be lying by the window, looking out at the chaos of Manhattan rather than experiencing it for herself."

That makes Matt chuckle. "Sorry I'm just asking

this now, but you distracted me. How did it go with Maggie today?"

"I distracted you? You were the one wearing nothing but a towel," I say with a laugh.

The back of his hand caresses my cheek, and he stares into my eyes, looking serious. "You're beautiful. You've been distracting me since the first day we spoke. Dating others didn't work. Being your friend didn't work. Being mad at you didn't work. This," he says as his hand moves south, "works much better."

"*She lets out a content sigh,*" I say, "*wondering how she got so lucky. How she ended up in this bed, with this man. The man of her dreams.*"

"Oh, are you writing our story now?"

"We're writing it together as we go, but I was just thinking of how I used to write perfect moments like this but never really experienced them myself."

"After you and Blake split up, you told me that you couldn't find a guy in college who lived up to your hopes and dreams, so you decided to write him."

"And in typical Matt fashion, you took that as a challenge? I remember you saying that maybe you should start reading my books. So that you could see how you measured up."

"And?" he says, pressing his lips—well, really, pressing his whole body against me along with his lips.

"You don't just measure up, Matt. You're better than even I imagined."

He throws one fist up in the air and yells out, "Ha! Hail to the victor!"

WE GET OUT of bed eventually and take a long, hot shower together. Then, we put on the matching hotel robes and order room service.

We're sitting in the living room, sharing minibar beers and taking in the setting sun, when I ask, "You know how we were talking earlier about writing the perfect guy?"

"Yeah."

"Oh, wait. I need to tell you about what happened with Maggie first. She seems resigned to the fact that she needs to take me seriously or she's going to lose me."

"Do you think she will make a good offer? The kind you want?"

"I hope so. I do really like working with her. Or at least, until recently, I did. I've thought a lot about what you said about publishing myself, and although I agree with you that I maybe could make more money and that I would be fully in control, I'm not sure I want to take on the responsibility of basically owning a publishing company. I want to have more free time to spend with you, not less."

"Makes sense," he says. "How did Maggie leave it?"

"She said she'd get back to me, but as soon as I

left, Blake called me."

"Ah, yes. The billionaire. Mr. Screw Up and Try to Fix It with a Million Roses."

"You almost sound jealous." I smirk at him. "He said he shouldn't be telling me but that Maggie was given a blank check to keep me."

"Wow. The billionaire might be my new best friend. Good thing I put this suite on your credit card."

My mouth drops open in mock horror.

"Just kidding," he says, rolling his eyes. "Keep going."

"I think it will all work out, but it's what he told me *after* that got me thinking. He met someone. He's taking time off, and he sounds happy. In my books, I gave all the guys I dated happy endings, and I can't help but wonder how they are doing now."

"Well, the whole world knows how rock-star asshole Dustin is," Matt says with a scowl. "And I do happen to know that Luke, your hockey player and my friend, is loving being a full-time professional. *And* get this: Ginger broke off her engagement with Mark not long after he broke his leg and is now engaged to Luke."

"Oh my God! No!"

"Well, she wanted to be a pro athlete's wife," Matt says, shrugging as he takes another sip of beer.

"Should we page Dr. Jake and see how he's doing?" I ask.

Matt nods, grabs his phone, and clicks around, pulling up Jake's social media, which causes me to tilt my head and stare at him.

"You might have cut off all ties, but I … okay, maybe I was slightly online stalking some of the guys you dated when you dated them. I told myself I was doing it to keep you safe. That kind of thing."

"That's the sweetest thing I think I've ever heard." I lean closer and give him a peck on the cheek.

"Shut up, Valentine," he says as he pulls up a photo and puts it in front of me. "Look at this."

This time, my mouth drops open from real shock. "He married his crazy ex, Erin? What was he thinking?!"

"Aw, look," Matt counters. "They had their dogs walk down the aisle before them."

"That is kind of cute," I admit. "Well, I hope they are gloriously happy together."

"Speaking of a gloriously happy married couple," Matt says, clicking away again. "Check this out."

There's a tabloid headline: *PAXTON CLEARY KICKS IT UP IN COWTOWN STRIP CLUB.* And there's a photo of Paxton with his arms around two voluptuous strippers while another gives him a lap dance.

I glance at the date. See the article is quite recent. "Still have an alert set up for news of him?"

"Yep. Let's just say, I liquidated our Cleary Oil stock holdings." He grins at me. "And have since turned the alert off."

"I wonder if he was telling the truth. If the marriage didn't mean anything."

"Looks like it."

"I feel bad for Lana actually. She wasn't nice to me at the party at their ranch, but now, I understand why. She was in love with him."

THE DOORBELL TO our suite rings, causing Phoebe to wake, suddenly on full alert. She doesn't bark, but she rushes to the door. Mostly because when the doorbell rings at Matt's place, it's because there is a food delivery that she wants in on.

I expect it to be room service. And it is, but Hayley is right behind the server and his cart.

"What are you doing here?" I say, causing the server to look confused. I point back at Hayley and then gesture him inside.

"I went to your place, and they told me you were here!" She's carrying two large paper bags. I see the top of a bottle of champagne sticking out of one.

A lightbulb switches on in my head. "Oh, Hayley. Oh, Hayley!"

"It went through! The transfer! It went through!"

I toss my arms around her, squealing and shrieking along with her.

"I'm so happy for you!" I say even though I want to cry my heart out at the thought of my best friend moving so far away.

"We were ready to give up hope."

Her cheeks are wet when I let go of her, which means we have something in common. I think a few tears are perfectly reasonable. So long as I can keep from falling on the floor and grabbing her by the ankles and begging her not to leave me.

Matt comes out and sizes up the situation as quickly as I did. "Hey, congrats! That's great news! Come on in." He looks and sounds genuinely happy as he takes the bags from her.

The waiter gets our food all set out on the dining room table and leaves, so Hayley starts adding what she brought to the mix. It's an odd array—sushi, bagels, and cheddar cheese popcorn.

"Are you having cravings already?" I say with a laugh.

"Maybe. I don't know. I was just hungry."

"Well, let's pop this champagne," Matt suggests, picking up one of the bottles. "And the sparkling cider."

"I know it's not the same, but—" Hayley says.

"Totally worth it," Matt says.

After we toast and take our seats, Hayley seems to finally notice our bathrobes. Our still-damp hair. "Oh my gosh. I didn't even think! I totally just interrupted you. I'm so sorry."

"It's okay. It's crunch time for the crew, so they kicked us out for a few days. We're going to have this amazing reveal of the project when it's all done," I tell her.

"And you'd be proud of Kitty," Matt tells Hayley. "She is going to be negotiating a new contract with the publisher—on *her* terms."

"That's amazing!" she says, shoving a vegetarian sushi roll into her mouth.

"I know! Blake told me he gave Maggie *carte blanche* in regard to me."

"Wait. You talked to Blake?" she asks.

"Yes," Matt answers for me. "Which led us down the rabbit hole. We were just playing Where Are They Now with all the guys she's dated."

"Oh, fill me in!" she says, deciding she's done with the sushi. She dishes up half of the pasta I ordered and starts working on it.

Matt catches her up on what we know so far, and she says, "So, fireman, actor, and best man are left. I have the scoop on the best man. Kellen Briggs has *moved to Tibet, where he hopes to find a better connection with the meaning of life*—or at least, that's what his parents told Zack and Kylie. In truth, he's in Thailand, gambling."

"That's too bad. You'd think practically dying over gambling debts would cure you of something like that. Or cause you to want to get help. But then again, I've never had an addiction," I say, feeling bad for Kellen.

"Let's do the fireman next," Hayley says. If I didn't know better, I'd think she was tipsy, but I think she's just really enjoying this moment of fun after all the stress she's been under. She punches a few buttons on her phone. "Oh," she says, looking concerned and then quickly scanning whatever she's reading. She looks up at me and says, "Bryce Nichols died from injuries sustained in duty. He was inside a burning home and aided the rescue of twin baby girls before the second story was overcome by fire."

Tears fill my eyes. "I'm very sad he's gone, but part of me feels strangely glad for him. He wanted to die a hero."

Matt reaches over and squeezes my hand.

Hayley grabs my other one, causing me to blurt out, "I'm so happy you're going, but I'm so sad you're leaving."

"That's just the thing," Hayley says. "We're not sure if we are."

"What?"

She looks at Matt, and they share some kind of knowing glance. I wonder what's up, but then she says, "Of course, I'm leaving in a few days, and I will be spending the holidays with Nicholas in California. But I listened to what you said the other day, about designing my life. And you were right. We're thrilled the transfer came through. It takes the pressure off. We're committed to being there at this point, but we've both put out a few feelers to other firms. We'll see. And since I won't see you for Christmas …" She pulls a small wrapped gift out of her bag.

"Oh, Hayley. I don't have my gift for you here with me."

"That's okay. This is just something little. I was hoping to give it to you before your negotiations, as a reminder, but it sounds like you earned it today."

I open the package and find a pretty bracelet with letter beads in the middle that spell out BADASS.

I get up off my chair and give her another hug. "This is amazing. I love it."

She stands up and says, "Well, I hate to eat and run, but I have to eat and run."

She pats Phoebe on the head and gives Matt a hug, and then she's off.

WE FINISH EATING, and then Matt says, "Wanna watch a movie?"

"Yeah, that sounds fun," I tell him. "Maybe a holiday one?"

He clicks on the television and scrolls through the channels. He stops when he sees Rafe's face on the preview screen. A reporter is sitting down across from him and a pretty girl, who I assume is his costar, based on where she's sitting next to Rafe in a pair of director chairs.

"Have you been scared during the filming?" the reporter asks the girl.

I remember that the lead role he got was for a horror film.

The girl reaches her hand over, squeezes Rafe's,

and says, "Not when I have him around."

"Oh," the reporter says, seeing television gold in front of her. "Are you two dating?"

"We're enjoying our time on set," Rafe says, obviously trying to be discreet. He's such a nice guy.

"I wouldn't call it dating," the girl says with a chuckle. "More like hooking up. Being scared all day makes you horny." She giggles and covers her mouth. "Oops. Can I say *horny* on television?"

"Well, we know what the actor is doing now," Matt says.

"More like *who* he's doing," I quip.

Chapter Nineteen

FOR THE SECOND day in a row, there's champagne in the forecast.

At least, that's what Maggie thinks. There's a bottle in a metal bucket next to her desk, just like there used to be in the old days, but today is different. I've got my *BADASS* bracelet on. And it makes me feel invincible.

"There she is!" She rushes over to me before I've barely taken three steps into her office. "My superstar."

Lois is behind me, and she very loudly clears her throat. "Cut the bullshit, Maggie, and let us sit down."

Maggie's cheeks match her red lipstick. "Of course. Let's sit down and enjoy some champagne."

"At ten in the morning?" Lois mutters just loud enough for me to hear.

I snort softly and exchange a look with her before we take our chairs in front of Maggie's desk.

There I am, still on the wall. The same framed news items covering my stellar career. *Gosh, I was naive back then.*

Lois follows my eyes and gives me a knowing look. But she can't smile. She's in negotiating mode, I can tell. And I have to wonder if Maggie can too. Hence the too-bright attitude. The champagne.

Maggie pops the cork and laughs softly. "We're on the verge of something big, ladies. Kitty Valentine is about to explode."

I look down at myself. "I hope not. It's been ages since I've had an excuse to get dressed up, and I'd hate to ruin this outfit. Not to mention, the shoes."

Her smile falters. "I wasn't speaking literally."

"Let's get down to business, shall we?" Lois cracks her knuckles. "We know you want another ten books. You probably know I've been talking to two other publishers on Kitty's behalf."

Maggie sighs before putting the champagne back on ice. "Yes. Word gets around."

"I'll save us both some time by cutting to the chase. What are you willing to offer?"

Dang. I might as well not be here.

The two of them stare each other down like a pair of warriors who aren't new to this field of battle.

Should I be recording this? I feel like I might want to go back and watch it again, maybe with Matt and Hayley and a lot of wine.

I have a momentary twinge of sadness at the realization that Hayley packed her bags and left for California this morning, so moments like that won't be happening like they used to.

Maggie's gaze slides away from Lois and lands on me. Her brow furrows. "Do you really want to go elsewhere? After everything we've been through?"

"That's not fair," I say.

"Isn't it?" She plops down in her chair. "I bent over backward to keep you here. To revitalize your career. You were tanking. Or don't you remember that?"

"So, what? I have no choice but to stay with you forever? You know I am grateful. If I wasn't, I wouldn't have continued with this trope-dating scheme for as long as I have. You know I've been unhappy with it."

"So, we'll stop it then. No problem." She shrugs, hands in the air. "It's done."

Lois and I exchange a look.

"Really?" I ask, and I don't bother hiding my skepticism. I think it's well earned after all the double-talk I've received lately. I don't know where I stand with her anymore. And I don't know if she is trying to play hardball and doesn't want me to know about Blake's blank check or if we just shouldn't be working together.

"Sure. I'll pass the word along that we're finished with that. You can still write trope-based, on-trend romance, but you don't have to go through with dating a new man for every book. There was only so long the arrangement could last. Everyone knew it."

Lois takes a sharp breath like she's ready to unleash something serious, but I cut her off with a pat on her hand.

"Funny. Not that long ago, you were determined to keep me dating. What's with the sudden change?" I ask, wanting her to level with me. Needing her to be honest.

"It's business, sweetie. This is how negotiation works."

She's not fooling me. Or Lois evidently. "More bullshit, Maggie. Come on. What happened? Did you hear how popular our girl is? Just figure out you aren't the only shop in town?"

"There was a meeting," Maggie says. "We looked over the sales figures and decided we have too good of a thing going with Kitty to let her go so easily." She looks at me. "If you don't think I fought for you, you don't know me at all. And that's a shame."

"I believe you would." That's the truth, though I'm still waiting to hear just how she fought and what that means. I don't think anybody could blame her for occasionally overinflating her worth, but it means taking what she says with a grain of salt sometimes.

"I made sure your freedom was something we could offer."

"What's that mean? My freedom?"

"You're free to write based on what's up here." She taps her temple. "You've already proven you have what it takes to write compelling, steamy romance. I made sure to remind everybody in that room how you rose to the occasion and revitalized your book sales by stepping outside your comfort zone. The least any of us can do now is give you a little breathing room."

I know better than to rejoice just yet. We're negotiating, like she said. This isn't the end of it.

"So, you're saying the publisher wants ten books. Trope-based, like before. But written without the need to date anybody new."

"Correct." She smiles, triumphant, and stops just short of asking me to congratulate her on a job well done.

Good thing since I'm not in any such mood. Not yet.

"What about the publicity stuff? I thought part of the reason they wanted me to stick to the tropes was to stay consistent with what everybody already knows. It got people excited. They want more. They want to imagine me dating the men I write about."

She purses her lips, and I know I've landed a blow.

"Well?" Lois prompts. I feel like I have to play nice, but my agent clearly didn't get the memo. "What's the catch? What do they want her to do this time?"

Maggie's shoulders creep up until they're around her ears. "They want her to pretend she's still dating around."

"No way." I look at Lois, eyes wide. "I'm not going to live some double life for the sake of PR."

"No one would ever need to know you have a boyfriend."

"Yeah, except for the fact that I'm still getting attention when I'm out in public. I went shopping recently and was approached twice. At a home improvement store. Like, a bookstore I could understand. A library. But I can't even go out to look at paint swatches without hearing the opinions of my readers and having my picture taken."

"That's a good thing," Maggie says.

"What happens when I'm not alone? What happens when I'm out to dinner with my boyfriend? What, is he supposed to pretend along with me? Like he's the guy I'm writing about this time? Or are we supposed to be nothing but 'good friends'?" I make air quotes around the words, not bothering to hide my sarcasm. "Maybe we're not allowed to go out in public together for the next year. Is that it? Should we hide?"

"All right—"

"No, it's not all right! Here you are again, telling me how I'm allowed to live my personal life. I won't let that happen. If these are your terms, I'm out."

Lois places a hand on my arm. "Is this nonnegotiable?"

"It's a deal-breaker," I reply.

Maggie stares at me, studies me. "You would

leave us if that was a condition of your contract?"

"I would walk out of this office and never look back. Like we've already established, there are two other publishers interested in landing me as one of their authors."

Lois folds her arms. "Your move."

"Fine." Maggie throws her hands into the air. "It's done. You don't have to pretend."

"Really?"

"Really."

"What's the catch?"

"No catch." A smile plays over her mouth. "Naturally, the marketing department would've enjoyed keeping things status quo. I reminded them you're the one who has to face rude, social media–obsessed fans who don't understand the meaning of boundaries. I told them what you told me about being harassed in public. I think they understood."

And I know she's lying. Straight up. She's the one who liked the fact that her marketing idea worked. But I know Blake spoke to either her or her boss. And I can name my terms. I probably should just tell her and Lois that and stop all this.

I look to Lois, ready to do just that, but she says to Maggie, "To be fully forthright, we don't care what you're offering. Our terms are this: Kitty will write whatever she wants, whenever she wants. No more than two books a year. If she chooses to write more than that, you will have a first look, and if you don't make an offer within sixty days, she is free to submit her work to other publishers or even self-publish if she chooses." Maggie's mouth moves like she's about to respond, but Lois continues, "Her personal life will remain her own, and her social media presence, or lack thereof, will be up to her. And this is important: you will never agree to marketing plans—book signings, readings, or interviews of any kind—unless Kitty is comfortable with them. Oh, and when you announce that you have signed her—if you are allowed to—the deal will be considered a *major* deal. Per book."

Maggie looks like she swallowed something unpleasant. "Excuse me?"

My agent pulls a folded piece of paper from her handbag. "Here are the numbers offered by those houses we spoke of earlier along with the phone numbers of the acquiring editors. They'll confirm what I've written down."

Poor Maggie. Her eyes go round. "You can't be serious."

"You aren't the only person who reviews sales figures, Maggie. I know down to the penny how much Kitty's books have grossed across all international markets and all major retailers. I've done my homework, in other words." Lois jabs a finger toward that piece of paper. "If she'd commanded that sort of advance on this series, she would've earned out her advance on every book. Even the new release coming out, already has enough preorders to earn out. When does that happen?

Ever?"

Maggie only lifts a shoulder, still staring at the figures Lois handed her.

"All right, all right." Maggie shoots daggers at Lois from over the top of the page. "You've won. Congratulations."

"No. *She's* won." Lois pats my knee.

It takes a second for the truth of what she said to sink in. I am getting everything I asked for. Of course, once we get the contract, Lois will need to go over it with a fine-tooth comb to make sure it's all correct, but this means I get to stay here if I want. And although I'm not thrilled with Maggie's treatment of me lately, I do like the fact that the man who literally holds the company's purse strings is a friend. I wouldn't have that connection anywhere else.

"Now"—Maggie goes back to the champagne bottle, fills three flutes, and hands one to Lois and me—"here's to Kitty!"

"Hear, hear," Lois agrees, downing her glass. She sets it on the desk and says, "I'd like to have a new contract on my desk by the end of the week."

Maggie nods in agreement, and Lois walks out the door. I feel like I should follow, but it seems a little abrupt. So, I take another sip of champagne.

"I'd love to talk with you, if you have a few minutes," Maggie says to me.

"Sure," I say, glancing at my watch. I'm not scheduled to meet up with Matt for another hour.

"What's up?"

"I need to level with you now that the negotiations are over. Now that Lois has left."

"Okay."

"My job has been in jeopardy. My business line revenue has been decreasing. I care about you, Kitty. You've been like the daughter I never had since the day you walked into my office. When you were a fresh-faced college girl with big dreams. I knew that the publishing industry could chew authors up and spit them out, just like any other big business could. I didn't want that to happen to you, and I've always tried to protect you from it. But it got to the point where I couldn't anymore. I'm sorry if I've been rude to you. I don't think you just sit at home and write and that it's easy. I was just under a whole lot of pressure. I was grasping at straws when I threw out the whole idea of the publicity tour. I never thought it would take hold. But it did. And then I couldn't get out of it. I felt trapped, like I'm sure you felt."

My posture has been stiff, and I feel like I've been on full alert since we walked in here, but what she said makes me relax a little.

"And I think you made the right decision for your personal life. I hope that we can continue to work together after all this. But if you would like to be assigned another editor, I'll understand."

This causes me to soften. In fact, I set my drink on her desk, walk up to her, and startle her by giving her a hug. "I really don't want a new editor. You understand how I work. My style. You're good at what you do."

"Thank you."

"And if it wasn't for you, honestly, I might still not have spoken to my hot neighbor."

"And now, you're together."

"Yes. Wanna hear the ultimate meet-cute for an author?" I ask her, taking a seat and making myself comfortable.

"Of course."

And then I tell her all about getting drunk, going across the hall, asking Matt what his favorite position was, and proceeding to strip naked and puke on his rug.

By the time I'm through, we're both rolling with laughter. And it feels good.

Chapter Twenty

I WAKE UP to Phoebe pawing me. I roll over toward Matt but find that he's not in bed. A glance at the clock tells me it's nine in the morning.

After all the excitement over the publishing deal yesterday, having lunch with Matt, shopping till we dropped for Christmas presents for our families, and then celebrating over dinner, I was exhausted and fell asleep quickly.

And I must have been tired.

Phoebe paws me again.

"What is it, girl? Where's your daddy?"

She runs toward the doorway and waits for me. I stretch, get up, throw on a robe, and go out to the living room, Phoebe leading the way.

I find Matt on his computer, sitting at the desk. The television is on, and stock market activity is running across the screen.

"What's going on?" I ask him.

He swivels the chair around to face me. And I have one of those moments. A moment where the simplest thing makes a huge impact on me. He's dressed in his normal athletic wear. But today, his face is clean-shaven. And while I love the scruff he let grow while we were kicked out of our bathroom, I realize he's even more handsome without it. And that's saying something. I think most every hero I write in a book has the *perfect amount of sexy scruff*. God, he has a pretty face. I touch my hair, knowing I probably look like a disaster, but for once in my life, I don't care.

Phoebe rushes up to him and gives him a nod. Like, *Task performed, master. She's up and moving.*

He scratches the top of her head. "She wants breakfast. I told her I couldn't order until Mommy woke up."

"*Mommy*?" I say, taking in a sharp breath.

"I, uh … sorry, I wasn't thinking," he says. "I don't know why I just said that."

"I would love to be Phoebe's mommy." Tears fill my eyes, causing the dog to rush over and lick my face.

"I think she wants your first task to be to order her some food," Matt says with a laugh.

But then our gazes meet. And lock. And I can see our entire future.

He gets out of his chair, walks to me, and kisses me fully on the lips. It's an emotion-filled kiss, and it gives me an immense amount of joy.

We get to the business of placing our room service order, and then Matt's cell phone rings. I assume it's a work call even though it's only a few days before Christmas. Three, to be exact. Nothing like cutting it close. Tomorrow is the 23rd. We're supposed to go to my grandmother's for Christmas Eve and then have her and Peter along with Matt's family, who I finally get to meet, to Christmas dinner at our place.

"Hey, Jack," Matt says when he answers his phone. "Uh-huh. Okay. I understand."

Crap. It was all going good until the *I understand* part.

I'm basically holding my breath, praying my holiday plans aren't about to go up in smoke. Although we do have a backup plan of holding both at Grandmother's, so it will all be okay. It will be beautiful whenever it takes place.

"That was Jack," Matt says.

"Uh-huh," I say, scarcely able to get the syllables out due to lack of oxygen.

"Tomorrow night. Nine o'clock."

"We get to see it tomorrow night? They are actually going to get it done?"

"Did you doubt me?"

"You?" I say, sauntering up to him and dropping my robe. "Although you were quite the sexy construction worker, you didn't do any of the work."

His eyes go straight to my chest. So do his hands. He raises his eyes at me just as the doorbell rings, causing Phoebe to go ballistic.

"Saved by the bell," I tease Matt, giving him a quick peck before pulling my robe back on and answering the door.

WE EAT BREAKFAST, and then I get dressed, so we can take Phoebe on a walk through the park. It's chilly and damp, and there's a chance of snow for Christmas. Everyone we pass seems to be cheerful.

At least, I know I am.

I'm officially a dog mom. And for some reason, it feels like an even bigger step than moving in together.

Although I think I know now how Matt met so many women. Phoebe seems to have a fan club that includes *everyone* she comes into contact with.

They all comment on what a pretty dog she is. How good she is. Her silky fur.

And I have to say, I feel damn proud.

When we get back, Matt tells me he's going out. And he's being very vague about it.

"Where are you going?" I ask again.

"I can't tell you that. It will ruin the surprise. And in case you forgot, you like them now."

"Dang it," I tease. "That's fine. I actually have a little shopping I need to do myself." And I do. I want to find the perfect outfit to wear for our first holiday together. I want to look gorgeous on Christmas Eve and approachable, friendly, and lovely on Christmas Day.

"I thought your shopping was done?"

"I thought it might be fun to have something new to wear. You know, to meet your family."

"They've never met you, so they haven't seen any of your clothes."

"I know that," I say, rolling my eyes.

"It's a girl thing, right?" he says.

"Exactly."

Chapter Twenty-One

"NINE O'CLOCK CAN'T come fast enough," I tell Hayley.

She has arrived in California and sounds deliriously happy to be back in Nicholas's arms.

"I can't wait to see it," she says.

"So, what do you think of California so far? Hate it?" I tease.

"I think I'd go anywhere with this man," she says in a dreamy voice.

And for the first time in my life, I totally understand. I feel the same way.

"Hey, you're with *Nicholas*," I say.

"Uh, yeah," she replies, sounding confused.

"And it's Christmastime."

"Uh-huh."

"You're with *your* sexy Santa. You have to make him dress up. I mean, he's *St. Nicholas*, right?"

"The man is probably going to have to be a saint to put up with me while I'm pregnant," she says. "I am having some cravings. But he says we should go for it. Enjoy all the fun parts of pregnancy. Did you know that during the first trimester, besides morning sickness, many women have an, shall we call it, enhanced libido?"

"I did not know that. Good for you."

I hear a horn honking in the background.

"Wow," I say. "If I didn't know better, I'd think you were in New York."

"No!" she replies. "It's just our Uber driver. We're going, uh, somewhere."

"Somewhere?"

"Yes. It's a surprise. St. Nick is surprising me," she says.

"Well, okay then. Have fun! But you should know that I'm making Matt take me out for nachos tonight before we go home."

"Cool," she says, practically hanging up on me.

I guess Santa couldn't wait.

I BOUGHT FOUR new outfits yesterday, complete with accessories, shoes, and a handbag. It's not something I normally do, but I feel like I need to look nice for my new house.

Like *I want it to have a good impression of me the first time we meet again* kind of thing.

I also possibly racked up some credit-card damage in the lingerie department. I'm talking *it's a whole new me* underneath my clothes. If I'm going to sleep in a gorgeous four-poster bed every night, I need to look the part.

"Stop pacing," Matt says, handing me a glass of wine. "You're making Phoebe nervous."

"I'm just so excited; I can hardly stand it."

"I have one more email to send. We'll go downstairs to the bar, get some nachos, have a drink, and then we'll come back up and get Phoebe. We'll be there before you know it."

I EAT MY weight in nachos—part in sorrow over Hayley not being here, part in excitement to be here with Matt, part in nervousness, and part because the nachos are damn good.

In situations like this, when I'm nervous, I normally drink. But I can't be drunk in my new space. It would set a bad tone, and I'd have to sage it or something and start over.

Matt checks his watch and finally says the words I've been waiting for, "We should probably cash out and go get our stuff."

"Ahhh!" I say, giving him a kiss.

THE FIRST THING that's very different is the fact that the door to my apartment is gone. Boarded up, drywalled, newly painted. I knew it was going to happen, but it stops me in my tracks. I touch the wall, feeling like I'm now lost.

"Weird, isn't it," Matt says, "not seeing your door?"

"Yeah, it is." I momentarily panic. "Are you sure we did the right thing?!"

He pushes me against the wall where my old door used to be and kisses me. Deeply.

"Absolutely," he says. "Just think, Kitty, we're about to walk into *our* home."

I'm nodding at him as emotional tears threaten when he suddenly picks me up, carries me to his— make that, *our*—front door, and turns the knob.

"You're carrying me over the threshold," I say, the tears fully flowing now.

"Of course I am. It's good luck. We don't wanna jinx this whole thing from the start."

He twirls me around, sets me down on my feet, and says, "Wow!"

And wow is a total understatement, yet I don't have the words to describe how this all looks. And I'm a writer. Words are what I do.

His kitchen and dining room look mostly the same, except there is a new dining room table and the holiday decor we had scrunched in there is spread out with more added. It looks incredible. The living room furniture is all the new stuff I picked out, but it looks better than I imagined. We chose to go with a kind of modern-loft feel but kept all the vintage charm of the apartment. Thick wood moldings surround every window and door. The baseboards, decorative crown, and coffered ceiling in the dining room used to be a medium wood tone that had a little too much yellow in it. It's all been painted bright white, which causes you to notice every single beautiful detail. The walls in the living room are a shade softer. The built-in bookcases that surround the fireplace have been painted a dark gray, and many of our favorite books and collecti-bles are displayed. *Together.* There's a blue silk rug with a subtle white pattern on top of the original restored herringbone wood floor. There are gold accents and rich colors, and the fireplace—*oh my God, the fireplace*—looks so different too. The mantel is still there, but the cracked green marble has been replaced with a gorgeous white marble with golden swirls. If I were writing a book right now, I'd have to go back and edit it because I know I'm rambling, but I can't even.

"We get to live here," I finally blurt out.

Phoebe jumps up on the new couch and rolls onto her back.

"Phoebe!" Matt says, but I just chuckle.

"She approves!" I say.

The apartment door opens, and Jack and his wife, Barbara, come in. "What do you think of the place?"

"We haven't gotten past this spot," Matt says. "I think we're both in shock."

"And to think, I used to make fun of people on those HGTV shows who would see their new house and say the same thing for every room. Like, *Ohhh myyy gosshhh.* Or, *Is this our house?* Or, What? Or crying about how beautiful it is or all the other things they say."

Barbara takes over, discussing all the details I can barely focus on. It looks so different. I mean, I thought both our places were nice before. This is just beyond.

"Now, to the new wing," she says, turning us toward the door to Matt's bedroom.

But there isn't just a door anymore. There's an arched entry. I recall something like this from the plan, but it's even prettier than I expected and adds more of that vintage charm.

She leads us into what I know used to be my apartment. My kitchen is gone, and in its place is a super-cool hangout space.

"The bar is an antique, from an old hotel in the city," she says, gliding her hand across the wood top before pointing around the room. "Your pool table. Big screen."

I look at Matt, who is grinning widely.

He's like me, mostly mute, but he does occasionally mutter, "Wow," or, "Cool." But he's excited about this room, and he and Jack are now behind the bar, talking about the built-in keg and the wine fridge. So excited that he barely gives a glance to his new, modern office space.

Barbara grabs my hand and points to a set of tall French doors. The doors are paned, but instead of see-through glass, like is typical, this is set with old mirrors, causing light to bounce around the room. She places me in front of them and says, "Open them up."

"*Ohhh myyy gosshhh*. Is this mine?" I ask, taking in the library that is like something from my dreams.

There are chairs for reading, blue bookshelves all the way to the top of the ceiling, and even my very own sliding ladder, so I can reach—and dust—all the books at the top.

I move to a window and recognize the view. "This is where my window seat was."

"You said it was one of your favorite spots in the house, and that's why we had to keep it. I updated the cushions with some extra fluff, new fabric, and pillows."

I spin in a circle. "This whole room is my favorite spot in the house!"

She grins at me. "Yeah, but you haven't seen the master suite yet."

"The master suite," I repeat dreamily. This whole thing seems like a dream.

Matt must have heard me speak because he's at my side and holding my hand. "Let's go check it out!"

We go back down the new hall and to another set of mirrored doors. Matt dramatically swings them open, revealing a cozy bedroom with our new four-poster bed. I know this is a combination of our two bedrooms, both of which were of good size, and I'm surprised this room seems a little small. Not too small. It's perfect, but I'm trying to figure out where all the space went. The bedroom portion is actually a little smaller than what we had before.

"Your retreat," she says, taking us around a corner where there are four doors. Two are his-and-hers highly organized closets.

"I'm obsessed with my closet," I mutter to no one in particular.

It's painted the same Tiffany blue as my office used to be, and it has white shelving with gold accents. Matt's closet is painted white with masculine dark cabinets.

Beyond that is our master bath. Although she was right when she called it a retreat. There's a modern free-standing tub and gold-accented tiles with a Moroccan flair, highlighting the fireplace wall behind it. Coordinating tiles fill the large steam shower, and I can feel the heated marble floor under my feet. His-and-her sinks and a makeup area for me complete the gorgeousness that is this room.

"I can't believe this all used to be my bedroom," I say.

I kind of thought I'd be sad to see it go. Kind of like when you get a new car and you feel bad for ditching your old one, but then you get in the new one and forget all about it. Actually, it almost reminds me of what it was like to spin the wheel and date the guy. Each one seemed shiny and new.

Matt puts his arm around me and kisses the side of my face, causing me to melt. Now, I know how people say they feel on their wedding day when they can't stop smiling.

I.

Cannot.

Stop.

Smiling.

"Last stop, your office," Barbara says.

"Oh crap. My office. I literally forgot about my office. It's where all the magic happens!"

"I certainly hope that's not the case, but maybe when we tire of the four-poster bed, baths in front of the fire, you spread out on the pool table, and that living room couch, we can give it a go."

"Matt!" My eyes get huge. "You can't say all that!"

"I was thinking it too," Jack says.

"Boys," Barbara says, rolling her eyes. "Kitty, see what you think."

She swings the door open, and what I see is not only beautiful with its barely blush walls, but it's also got a funky, creative vibe. A fabric bulletin board hangs above my desk, perfect for pinning up inspirational pictures. I didn't do it in the trope books, but when I wrote my sweet romances, one of my favorite things to do was peruse real estate listings to find the characters the perfect homes. My character development went from simple physical characteristics to deciding on their favorite colors and foods. The cars they drove. How they kissed. My old desk is here, but it's been paired with a chair that will be more comfortable and supportive for hours with my butt in it. New bookshelves line one wall with copies of all my books in both English and foreign language editions. There's a daybed for naps and big gold letters that spell out *Kitty*.

I rush to Barbara and throw my arms around her. "It's so amazing. Everything is incredible. And I can't believe you managed to do this so fast."

"We had a big crew, and honestly, after this experience, I think it's going to be our thing. We realized people don't have the time or energy to live through six months of renovations, so we're going to start doing more of these. They're fun and rewarding."

"And thank you for decorating for Christmas. It will be my first time meeting Matt's family. And I just wanted …" Crocodile tears fill my eyes.

"It to be perfect," she finishes for me.

THEY OPEN A bottle of champagne, do a toast with us, and then leave us in our home. Matt walks out, and when he comes back in, he's carrying a couple of wrapped packages.

"What's that?"

He grins at me. And my gosh, does he look sexy doing it. Maybe the new place has me all hyped up on adrenaline or nesting hormones or something, but all I can think about is ripping his clothes off.

"I have a couple surprises for you. Early presents."

"Early presents. But I didn't—"

"Okay, fine," he says. "They aren't presents. Call them a holiday housewarming gift."

I consider this. "I can agree to that."

He leads me over to our new couch and takes a

seat. Phoebe, who got bored with the tour and took up her normal spot in her bed by the fireplace, all of a sudden is interested in the packages. Probably thinks it's food, knowing her.

Matt hands me a box wrapped in black paper. At first, that seems odd, but then I see the pattern on it. There are little kitties all over it, wearing Santa hats.

I open the present, careful not to rip the cute wrapping paper. Inside is what appears to be a long-sleeved white shirt. On it is a circle of gold and the words *A Very Kitty Christmas*. And inside that is a picture of a cute kitten peeking out of a red package under a Christmas tree.

"A very *Kitty* Christmas, huh?" I ask, loving the play on words.

"Yep," he says, "but don't think it's all about you."

"Well, my name is Kitty."

His hand moves up under my skirt, and his fingers graze my thigh before taking a swipe at my underwear. "And you have a very lovely kitty."

"Matt!"

He smirks at me, but anytime he touches me, my body flushes, my heart races, and my lady bits heat up.

He gently sets the next package on my lap. It's wrapped in red paper with a red ribbon, much like the one on the shirt.

I undo the ribbon, and the lid comes right off, as

it was wrapped separately.

Matt reaches into the box and pulls out something furry, and my first thought is that he bought a stuffed animal.

But then its head moves, and the kitten looks up at me. I notice its little pink nose as it yawns. It's a gorgeous tabby cat, multiple shades of orange, brown, and white. And there is a red bow tied around her collar.

I look at Matt in question and then glance from the shirt to the kitten and back again.

"I had her portrait done to put on the shirt," he says.

He what? How did he do that?

"How long have you had her?"

"Jack and Barbara have been keeping her at their house for me." He puts the little sweet furball into my arms.

"She's precious."

Phoebe paces around me, not sure what to think, but I notice that the fur on the back of her neck isn't standing up like it does when she hears the UPS truck. She's more curious. She puts her nose in the kitten's face, and the kitten playfully bats it away.

"She needed a good home, and she was just so cute that I couldn't say no."

"Did she not have a good home?" I ask, worried.

"She was very loved by her owner. She's a client of mine. Someone who I worked with when I was first starting out in the business. And even though I don't do private investing anymore, I still handle her portfolio. She is getting along in age and recently took a fall."

"Oh no!"

"She's fine. Just a broken wrist, but it was a wake-up call, and she decided to move into a senior living center—partly so someone can keep an eye on her, but also because she thought the social side of it would be fun. The only thing that was stopping her was that the new place doesn't allow pets. She asked me if Phoebe would like a cat sister. And I thought you would love her. A kitty for my Kitty."

WE FINISH THE champagne while I play with the kitten until she's tired. She goes over and lies right on Phoebe's bed with her, tucking herself under Phoebe's chin.

"Look at this. A dog and cat sleeping together," I tell Matt. "We're going to have to come up with a name for her."

"Well," Matt says, "she already has a name, but we can change it if you want."

"What is it?"

"Maggie," he says.

"Oh my God. Like my editor?"

"Happy coincidence, I'm afraid, but it is kind of fitting, don't you think?"

"Maggie it is."

Chapter Twenty-Two

"WOW! LOOK AT the snow coming down!" Matt says.

It's Christmas Eve. I'm dressed and ready to go to Grandmother's house, and I'm starting to get worried that the roads might get bad.

Matt is sitting in front of the fireplace. Kitty Maggie is playing with the ribbons on the presents under the tree, and I don't know if dogs can actually roll their eyes, but Phoebe might be doing so right now. She likes the kitten, but I think that maybe she didn't realize the cat would be staying.

"This is kind of a present," I tell him, picking up a gift and handing it to him. "It's sort of from Hayley. Mostly Hayley. And me."

He raises his eyebrows at me when he opens the package to find a spinning wheel.

"It's what Hayley made me. What I would spin to decide who to date."

"You two are crazy," he says.

"I know, but it worked. Now, I'm done. No more spinning the wheel. No more dating different guys."

"Well, I would hope so since we tore down the wall and everything."

"No more writing the books," I say to him seriously.

"Wait. I don't get to get dressed up anymore?"

"Oh, you most certainly do. That's why I'm giving you this. Thought you could keep it in the bedroom, spin it occasionally, and keep things fun."

He spins the wheel a few times and reads the tropes. "*Professor. Police. Bad Boy. Lifeguard. Foreign Lover*—oh, this will be fun, Kitty," he says in a fake accent. "I'm keeping this in my nightstand. You'll never know who you might come home to."

"As long as all of them are *you*," I say, throwing my arms around his neck and kissing him.

"Interesting," Matt says, which is an odd thing to say as he hands me a gift. "This is from me, but Hayley made it."

I find another wheel. "What?" But then I spin it and find the words *French Maid*. Another spin reveals *Librarian*.

He grins. "What's good for the goose is good for the gander…"

"I love it," I say with a laugh. But then get serious again. "But I didn't give you the wheel for that—unless you can inspire me to write more of these." I hand him a book. The book I wrote about him. And Phoebe. *Candy-Coated Love.*

He looks at me in confusion. "I already read this."

"And you already know it's based on you and Phoebe. It's a sweet romance with a happy ending—actually, that's not true. It ends with a sweeping big, fat happily ever after."

"You want one of those for yourself," he says knowingly. Then, he turns to Phoebe and says, "Go get your present."

Phoebe picks up something from her basket full of toys, brings it over, and drops a squeaky toy shaped like a bottle of champagne with the words *Dog Perignonn* in my lap.

"This is cute. But I don't get it."

"It's Phoebe's way of telling you that it's time for champagne."

He hops up and grabs a hidden champagne bucket with a bottle of the real stuff and two glasses.

When he sits down, he says, "Your grandmother says flutes are uncouth and a *coupe* is the only proper glass to drink bubbly from. Did you know this glass was first used in the '20s and it was modeled after the shape of a woman's breast?"

"I did not know that," I say, although if anyone knew that, it would be Matt.

"Neither did I until Peter told me," he says, causing me to giggle as he pops the cork and pours us each a glass.

"What shall we toast to?" I ask.

"Shoot," Matt says. "Phoebe, come back. You forgot something."

The second he says her name, she comes rushing back over, wagging her tail so hard that she almost knocks a book off the coffee table.

Matt holds her by the collar, and it's then I notice something dangling from it.

A small box.

He unclips it and hands it to me.

"This is from both of us," he says.

I inhale sharply, holding the breath in.

The box is … the right size.

No, Kitty, don't let your imagination go there. It's probably a dog tag with our new combined address on it.

But when I open the lid, a flash of light catches my eye. Glimmering in the box is a beautiful diamond ring. And when I look up, Matt has gotten up from his position, lounging on the rug, and is on bended knee in front of me.

Tears fill my eyes.

Because I know. I know this is finally that moment I've written so many times. That perfect moment when time stops and your life begins anew.

"Kathryn Antoinette Valentine, I think I've loved you since the day you literally stumbled into my life. And I want more than anything to be your endgame. I don't want our happy ending to be the end of the story. I want you happily living with me forever as my partner, my wife, my love. Will you marry—"

He doesn't get the words out before I launch

myself at him, throw my arms around his neck, and kiss him.

Tears are streaming down my face, incredibly happy ones, but we're alone, there's a fire, and we're on a new, soft rug.

No reason there can't be a little sexy times in our happy ending.

QUITE A WHILE later, we're still on the rug, our limbs tangled together, as Matt runs lazy little kisses down my neck. "You know, you never answered the question," he says. "Did you just use me for sex, and now, you're going to leave me?"

"Hardly."

He laughs. *"Hard* or hardly?"

"I'd say, it was a little of both," I tease.

I sit up, pulling a throw around my naked chest, and look down at him. He looks so beautiful, lying there. My *hot neighbor* Matt. My *future husband* Matt. My *forever* Matt.

I often write about those three little words—*I love you*—and I treat them like they are the most powerful words in the game. But I don't think I've ever really grasped how much more powerful *four* little words can be—*Will you marry me?*

"Yes," I say.

He takes the ring out of the box and slips it on my finger, sealing the deal.

"Do you like it?" he asks, his eyes landing on the ring.

"It's breathtaking. The stone is different. So simplistic. So large."

"It's an old cut. A rose cut," he says, sliding his hand across mine. "The stone is vintage."

"Vintage?"

"Yes, but the setting is new. Designed for you. By me. With a whole lot of input from Hayley and your grandmother."

"Wait. They know? And they kept it from me?" My eyes are wide, and I'm so shocked.

"They do. In fact, they've been waiting outside all this time for me to propose. Probably getting a little cold out there with the snow and whatnot. Especially since you attacked me." He grins.

"Matt!"

He smirks at me.

"Oh, I hate you." I swat my hand through the air in his direction.

He grabs it and pulls me close. "No, you don't. Because you just promised to love me forever."

"Um, no. Technically, I agreed to marry you. That's where the forever comes into play."

"Either way, we should celebrate." He pours us each another glass of champagne. "To us," he says.

And, well, I have to drink to that.

But as soon as I'm done, he takes my glass away and says, "We have to get dressed."

"Why?" I say, lying back down. "I'm so perfectly happy being naked."

"Because it's Christmas Eve and we're celebrating with your grandmother and Peter?"

"Oh shoot, that's right!"

I get myself back into my new, festive dress and am ready to go in record time. A look in the mirror reflects a girl who is insanely happy. And who can't wait to share the news.

Even though I suppose they already technically know.

"Can I call Hayley?" I ask once we're loaded into the black town car that was waiting at the curb. One that, apparently, Grandmother has had ordered for us—and by us, I mean, me, Matt, Phoebe, Maggie the cat, and our shopping bags full of gifts.

WE GET ALL of us and all our stuff into the foyer, set it down, and step into the great room.

"Surprise!" a bunch of people yell out.

And one of them is Hayley. She throws her arms around me, tears streaming down her face. "Not to steal any of your thunder," she says, "but not only am I here"—she holds up her left hand in front of her face—"but I just got engaged too!"

"This is the best Christmas Eve ever. Wait. What are you doing here? You were in California."

"I lied."

I give Nicholas a hug and congratulate him. Everyone is here. Kylie and Zack. Lois and Maggie both make an appearance. Grandmother and Peter are thrilled for us.

We are toasted to and honored by their love.

A few minutes before we're supposed to sit down for dinner, the doorbell rings.

Matt excitedly drags me to it and opens the door.

"Kitty, meet my family," he says, ushering them in. "Family, meet Kitty, my fiancée."

Matt's family is wonderful, and they fit right in. Of course, they knew he was proposing, like everyone but me. His parents are gracious, and I can already tell that my grandmother loves them. Of course, the fact that they are all handsome like Matt and well dressed with good manners doesn't hurt. Besides his parents, Michelle and Edward, there's his brother, Mark; his wife, Shelly; and their two kids, Lucy and Paul.

We have a delicious celebratory meal, and I float through the night on a cloud of happiness mixed with a lot of toasts with champagne.

AFTER DINNER, GRANDMOTHER pulls me aside.

"I want to tell you about your ring," she says.

That causes me to sit down quickly on the couch next to us.

"Well, the stone anyway. The stone was my grandmother's, who, at a time when marriages were often arranged, married for love. They lived a long and happy life together, and she bore three daughters and five sons. Her husband was a bit of a gambler and started a business at the right time, and they became fabulously wealthy. He gave her this diamond for their thirtieth wedding anniversary. When Matt came and asked me for your hand in marriage—"

"He did that?"

"Of course he did. I offered to pay for your ring. He refused, as I had known he would, so I offered him this stone. Told him he could have it set however he wanted. He liked the fact that the stone didn't look like all the other diamonds he had been looking at and said it was perfect for you. The rest is history." She takes my hand in hers and examines the ring. "The setting is beautiful. Simple and stunning. Just like you." Her eyes get teary, and just when I think she's about to get more emotional, she says, "So, have you set a date yet? You must start planning the wedding."

"Actually, Grandmother," I say, "I was thinking that we could start planning it."

"Oh, Kitty," she says, covering my hand with hers.

I can tell she's touched, and I'm pretty touched by the fact that for the first time in my life, she called me what my mother had—*Kitty.*

THE NEXT MORNING, I wake up next to Matt in our beautiful, new bedroom in our four-poster bed. I don't really remember getting into bed. I was exhausted from the festivities and the rush of all that had happened.

I pull my left hand out from under the covers and check to see if last night was real.

I'm happy to report that the ring is still there.

And this spring, I'm going to marry my hot neighbor. But I'm not going to write a book about it.

I don't think.

ABOUT THE AUTHOR

Jillian Dodd is the *USA Today* best-selling author of more than thirty novels.

She writes fun romances with characters her readers fall in love with—from the boy next door in the *That Boy* trilogy to the daughter of a famous actress in *The Keatyn Chronicles* to a spy who might save the world in the *Spy Girl* series.

She adores writing big fat happily ever afters, wears a lot of pink, buys too many shoes, loves to travel, and is distracted by anything covered in glitter.